## "Grif, I saw the ghost! He really exists!"

Nickie's eyes were frightened as her body pressed against his. His brain commanded his hands to let go of her arms, but they wouldn't cooperate. He found himself caressing her smooth skin with his curious, wayward palms, moving them up and down in a slow rhythm. "Okay," he capitulated, "what do you expect me to do about it?"

Her brown eyes widened as she met his gaze and read the unmistakable message there. "Well, not *that*."

"Why not that?" he coaxed, pulling her even closer. His flesh felt as though it were on fire.

"Well, I have to admit that terror and passion do have some things in common—pounding heart, sweaty palms, heavy breathing...."

"So why don't we take advantage of the adrenaline? I promise to give your ghost a run for his money."

## ABOUT THE AUTHOR

Lynn Lockhart can't pinpoint the exact moment she decided to be a writer as well as a reader, but once she set her first words on paper, she never looked back. That love of books led her to a master's degree in library science. Although she didn't realize it at the time, her first glimpse of the splendor of Versailles while on a college trip to France was so unforgettable, it planted the seed that eventually blossomed into *Nickie's Ghost*. She now makes her home in Florida with her husband, four cats and two dogs.

## Books by Lynn Lockhart

### HARLEQUIN AMERICAN ROMANCE
498—DATE WITH AN OUTLAW

Don't miss any of our special offers. Write to us at the following address for information on our newest releases.

Harlequin Reader Service
P.O. Box 1397, Buffalo, NY 14240
Canadian address: P.O. Box 603,
Fort Erie, Ont. L2A 5X3

# Lynn Lockhart

## NICKIE'S GHOST

# *Harlequin Books*

TORONTO • NEW YORK • LONDON
AMSTERDAM • PARIS • SYDNEY • HAMBURG
STOCKHOLM • ATHENS • TOKYO • MILAN
MADRID • WARSAW • BUDAPEST • AUCKLAND

If you purchased this book without a cover you should be aware
that this book is stolen property. It was reported as "unsold and
destroyed" to the publisher, and neither the author nor the
publisher has received any payment for this "stripped book."

For Robert, now and always

ISBN 0-373-16527-7

NICKIE'S GHOST

Copyright © 1994 by Marilyn Jordan.

All rights reserved. Except for use in any review, the reproduction or
utilization of this work in whole or in part in any form by any electronic,
mechanical or other means, now known or hereafter invented, including
xerography, photocopying and recording, or in any information storage
or retrieval system, is forbidden without the written permission of the
publisher, Harlequin Enterprises Limited, 225 Duncan Mill Road,
Don Mills, Ontario, Canada M3B 3K9.

All characters in this book have no existence outside the imagination of
the author and have no relation whatsoever to anyone bearing the same
name or names. They are not even distantly inspired by any individual
known or unknown to the author, and all incidents are pure invention.

This edition published by arrangement with Harlequin Enterprises B. V.

® and TM are trademarks of the publisher. Trademarks indicated with
® are registered in the United States Patent and Trademark Office, the
Canadian Trade Marks Office and in other countries.

Printed in U.S.A.

# *Prologue*

"Dominique Marie DuPrés! Get that filthy old doll off my Louis XIV table. Mary just waxed it."

"Yes, ma'am." Nickie winced at her great-aunt's harsh command, but she picked up Samantha and moved away from the undeniably glistening wood table that sat on the small landing between the first and second floors.

In her entire family, only Aunt Marie-Claire ever called her by her full name, and the way she barked it out, giving it a sharp French pronunciation, had Nickie hating everything connected with her ancestry. She knew her family was descended from an aristocratic line who had fled the guillotine to come to America, but at eleven years old, she didn't see it as a major factor in her life the way Marie-Claire DuPrés apparently did.

"Straighten your shoulders. Don't slouch like that." Her aunt reached down to poke her sharply in the middle of her back as she passed, causing her to flinch. "You'd never know that you have the royal blood of the Comte de Provence in your veins even if it has become watered down over the years.'' Marie-Claire drew a deep breath, lifting her chin and throwing her head back proudly. ''He later became Louis XVIII of France, you know.''

''Yes, ma'am.''

According to Nickie's mother, there was no real proof for this claim of kinship; she insisted it was only pretentiousness on Marie-Claire's part. Nickie wasn't sure exactly what that meant, but she realized that her great-aunt was unlike anyone else she'd ever known. Still, she didn't care about bloodlines, royal or not, although she was too polite and too much in awe of this relative of her father's to do more than secretly make a face behind the curtain of her dark brown hair. Clutching Samantha to her chest, she peered back over her shoulder just in case that bony finger was still lurking.

Marie-Claire gave a ladylike sniff when she saw the little girl's wary expression. ''Never mind. I'm not used to having children in the house. Why don't you go outside? It's a beautiful summer day.''

''There's no one to play with,'' Nickie wailed with mournful eleven-year-old logic.

The older woman fussed with the delicate lace ruffles that framed her throat. ''I'm sorry, young lady, but you'll just have to do the best you can. I'm sure it's better than remaining cooped up in the house. Your parents will be here to retrieve you on Tuesday.''

Nickie clutched the doll even more tightly as she dutifully complied, dragging her feet as she descended the stairs, her entire posture broadcasting her boredom and unhappiness. Retrieve indeed, she thought sourly, as though she were some kind of package to be picked up at the post office. She pushed open the front door and stepped onto the veranda.

Once outside the beautiful old mansion, Nickie found her feet automatically heading toward the arbor in the backyard. As she walked across the thick carpet of grass, she tilted her head back to gaze at one of the small dormer windows that marked the attic, wishing she could play there, instead of being banished outside.

She had discovered the attic yesterday when she was supposed to have been napping, and it was as though she had stumbled through the looking glass. The place was a veritable wonderland of old treasures just waiting to be uncovered, each item more magical than the last.

Time had become a meaningless blur until her aunt had suddenly swooped down on her like an avenging angel, alerted to her location because Nickie hadn't been able to resist trying out the squeaky old rocking horse in the corner. Marie-Claire had immediately and harshly forbidden her young charge to return to that part of the house, even going so far as to lock the door with a rusty old key, which she then dropped into the pocket of her dress.

In spite of her aunt's grudging hospitality and obvious inexperience in dealing with children, Nickie loved the elegantly furnished rooms and beautiful mirrored corridors of Bellefleur. As she settled herself on a shady stone bench, she childishly imagined that the place returned her feelings. She gazed up at the leafy canopy of trees, amazed at the noisy clamoring of the birds. She had never seen so many in one place; they seemed to come in all colors, shapes and

sizes, their cheerful chirping and fluttering wings filling up the loneliness of the afternoon. It was funny
how they always clustered at the back of the house.

She was following the antics of a beautiful red-
headed woodpecker that poked industriously at an old
gnarled limb, searching for bugs along the tree bark,
when she saw the man in the upstairs window. He
seemed to be leaning one shoulder against the window frame as he gazed wistfully out at the birds. His
hair was dark and combed back from his pale forehead in a style that seemed foreign to her young eyes,
as did the fit of his white high-necked collar. She
couldn't remember her aunt mentioning that she was
expecting company, but then grown-ups often did
things like that.

The man turned his head in her direction, although
from this distance she couldn't be sure he was actually looking at her. She stared up at him, deciding that
the windowpane must be dirty, because he appeared to
waver and ripple on the other side of the glass like a
bad TV picture. Or maybe it was the afternoon sunlight playing tricks on her eyes.

In any case, she knew without a doubt that he was
sad, as though he were a prisoner in a tower, locked
there by the spell of an evil witch. Her great-aunt certainly qualified for that category, Nickie thought with
a giggle. Hoping to cheer up someone who might be a
fellow prisoner, she smiled and waved to him. He
looked startled, hesitating for a moment before he returned her gesture with a graceful little bow.

Nickie was so delighted she stood up and curtsied in
return, giggling all the while. "Did you see that, Samantha?" she asked the doll who sat serenely wide-

eyed on the bench where Nickie had placed her. "He bowed to me just like the Prince did to Cinderella!"

When she looked up again he was gone.

Nickie sighed and shrugged and went back to watching the birds. Although she kept peering up at the second-floor window for the rest of the afternoon, to her acute disappointment, the sad man didn't reappear.

Later that evening she asked her aunt about his identity.

Marie-Claire looked at her sharply. "What man?"

"He was watching the birds from that room on the second floor, the one that has the desk with the owl lamp on it."

"What nonsense!" her aunt retorted. She dabbed at her lips with her napkin, her movements uncharacteristically jerky.

"But I saw him. He waved to me."

"What did he look like?" Marie-Claire demanded in her usual imperious manner.

Nickie tried her best to describe him, although it was difficult for her to put into words the desperate longing she had sensed in him. She could see that although her aunt pretended to be absorbed in cutting another perfectly proportioned bite of the sole meunière the cook had prepared, she was listening very carefully to every word Nickie uttered.

"What was he doing?" Marie-Claire asked.

"Nothing. He just looked sad, like he wanted to go outside. Why can't he go outside? Is he sick?"

"No one's sick around here." Marie-Claire's mouth thinned as she looked down her nose at her young grandniece for the longest time. "It must have been the gardener,'' she finally stated in the kind of grown-up voice that Nickie had learned meant the subject was closed.

Nickie frowned as she poked her fork at the piece of fish on her plate. With the sure instincts of a child, she knew Marie-Claire was lying. Beyond the fact that both men had dark brown hair, the man in the window looked nothing like the gardener, who was probably as ancient as her great-aunt. And what would Harry McInnis be doing upstairs in Bellefleur, anyway? He had his own snug house across the lawn where he lived with his family, not to mention the keys to the large shed where he kept all his tools and supplies.

Oddly enough, after this incident Marie-Claire went out of her way to be pleasant for the rest of Nickie's short visit. She even snapped a picture of her grandniece standing shyly but proudly on the steps of the front porch.

# Chapter One

*Bellefleur, Present Day*

The sound of a particularly raucous bird outside the open window caused Nickie to look up from the drawing of a desert fringe-toed lizard she'd been working on all morning. Her face broke into a grin as she gazed around the elegant second-floor study, her eyes taking in the soft green-and-gold hues of the flocked wallpaper, the gloss of the wood trim and the faded though still lovely green-and-buff carpeting. She wasn't yet able to believe that she was really here, at Bellefleur, and that the house now belonged to her because Marie-Claire DuPrés had bequeathed it to her in her will.

Never in her wildest dreams had she supposed she would be living in the house she'd adored as a child. In spite of her fussy and forbidding great-aunt, Nickie had felt a strong, unbreakable bond with this place, and although she knew she was being fanciful, she couldn't resist entertaining the whimsical notion that Bellefleur had somehow returned the sentiment by calling her back.

Even after all the years away, it still seemed like the only real home she had ever known, and she had settled in as quickly as a long-lost friend. So strong was her sense of belonging that even now she swore the house was looking over her shoulder in friendly approval as she sat at the lovely Queen Anne desk with its view of the gardens.

The interior of the mansion itself had been lovingly cared for both by her aunt and all those who had gone before her. The only immediate problem on Nickie's horizon was the care of the gardens. Nickie knew nothing about gardening and certainly had no idea how one went about caring for something as magnificent as those on this estate. Harry McInnis had apparently retired around the time her great-aunt had died, and there'd been no one to care for them since. They'd become somewhat run-down, like nobility gone to seed. She couldn't let them molder into further ruin, but she had no idea where to begin searching for a reputable gardener.

She still found it odd and rather intriguing that not long after that memorable visit she had paid to Bellefleur as a child, Marie-Claire had come up with the idea that the estate needed extensive gardens—the kind a palace might boast, with formal walkways lined with statues and a splashing fountain. So she had drafted her own gardener to take on the project. Harry had known little about executing such an elaborate design, which was probably why it had taken him more than ten years to complete the daunting task.

According to her great-aunt's lawyer, Harold Cohen, the entire layout covered more than ten acres. One of the first things Nickie had done after her arrival was inspect the grounds. It had almost made her giddy, this heady taste of what life as a royal must be like, as she'd walked along gravel pathways past rows of classical statues with their obviously allegorical meanings. She had suddenly felt more like a caretaker than an owner when she came upon the pièce de résistance, a large rectangular pool that boasted a statue of Neptune carrying a trident. Alongside him was a female figure, perhaps his consort, wielding a scepter. The fountain hadn't been turned on in over a year, and the shallow murky water in the pool glinted green in the sunlight.

Nickie bit her lip thoughtfully as she recalled the sense of awe and freedom she'd experienced as her feet had unconsciously traced the geometrical precision of the overall design. She glanced down at her drawing, tapping the paper with her eraser. It was difficult to pull her mind away from romantic gardens and allegorical statues to such a mundane subject as lizards, but it had to be done. Just as she leaned forward to add another reptilelike wrinkle to the creature's back, a sharp knock sounded at the front door.

She hurried downstairs, clutching the polished wooden banister as she made the turn to the landing. When she finally arrived at the bottom, she saw a woman standing on the other side of the screen door, her back to the house.

"Yes?"

The woman turned around to reveal that she was holding a plastic ice-cream container. "Well, hello, dear," she said in a warbly voice that reminded Nickie of a parrot. Even though the woman had to be sixty-five, her hair was jet black and carefully combed into what Nickie could only describe as a beehive with three large curls in the front. "You must be Dominique. I'm Velma Dare and I live in the big white house down the road."

"Hello. Won't you come in?" She held open the screen door politely.

"Don't mind if I do. I haven't been in the place since Marie-Claire kicked me out, and that's been more than ten years. Here." She thrust out the container and Nickie automatically reached for it. "It's homemade vegetable soup. It's not as good as when I use the vegetables from my garden, but it'll do. I don't suppose you have any iced tea made."

"As a matter of fact I do." Nickie smiled at the woman's frank request. She'd noticed that people in this small town were friendly and direct, quite a switch from the places she'd lived in while growing up. "Have a seat and I'll get us both a glass."

She hurried into the kitchen, setting the soup on the counter while she reached for a couple of glasses. When she turned around she found that Velma had followed her.

"Well, Dominique, the place hasn't changed a bit. It's an awfully big house for one person to rattle around in. Which is what I always said to your great-aunt, but she just sniffed at me in that superior way of hers. How are you settling in, honey?"

"Um . . . well—"

"Don't worry," she interrupted. "I call everybody 'honey.' It's just a habit of mine. Thanks." This last came as Nickie handed her a frosty glass of iced tea.

"It's not that." She tilted her head with a shrug. "It's just that everyone calls me Nickie."

"All right, honey. Nickie it is."

"I'm settling in fine," Nickie said as she led the way to the front living room.

"That's good." Velma never missed a beat, hovering close on Nickie's heels while her stream of words continued its effortless flow. "I restrained myself from bolting over here right off the rail. I told myself I'd better wait a couple of days and let you get your bearings. I didn't want to impose on you too soon, but I also didn't want you to feel neglected. Will your husband be joining you?"

"I'm not married," Nickie replied. She found herself drawing a deep breath, for Velma's sake, although the older woman didn't seem to need one.

"I see." Velma nodded with obvious approval. "I heard that Griffin McInnis is coming sometime soon."

"Yes, he's supposed to arrive today." Nickie couldn't help grinning at her neighbor's cheerful way of jumping from subject to subject. She gestured the other woman into one of the silk-brocade chairs while she settled into a corner of the couch. It looked as though it was going to be a thorough visit, but Nickie quickly assured herself that she needed a break from her scaly lizard friend upstairs.

"He's a former student of mine," Velma was explaining. "Tall, dark and handsome as sin and always good in math. Do you know what he wants?"

"According to the estate lawyer, he wants to search for some things he thinks his grandfather left in the cottage."

"What kind of things?"

Nickie smiled at her unabashed curiosity. "Mostly books, I think."

"Oh. Well, he won't stay long, that's for sure. Griff was never the type to be much interested in settling down." Velma chuckled. "A woman's worst nightmare, eh?"

Nickie smiled and shrugged, thinking of her own peripatetic life-style up to this point. "Perhaps."

"He's an engineer. Builds bridges and roads and such all over the country. When one job's over he packs up and moves on to the next. Seems to like it that way." Velma took a moment to cluck her tongue, whether in pity or indignation, Nickie couldn't tell. Then she was off again on another tangent. "Are you going to stay here permanently, or were you planning on selling the place?"

Nickie wasn't insulted by her inquisitiveness. In fact, she rather enjoyed it. She was an only child, the daughter of a father who had been transferred from one state to another because of his job as a salesman. They had never stayed more than five years in any one location, and they'd always lived in an impersonal suburb where the neighbors, although cordial, usually kept to themselves. Add to that the fact that her family was small and not especially close-knit, and she had never known the feeling of truly belonging.

Which was another reason she'd been thrilled to learn of her unexpected good fortune. None of her friends in Boston could understand why she was so intent on living at Bellefleur, not even after she showed them her treasured photograph of the house with her eleven-year-old self standing so proudly on the porch steps. They were even more baffled by her wanting to move away from the city to some godforsaken place in Tennessee that didn't even boast access to an ocean.

"I'm not going to sell," she replied with more force than the question warranted. "I intend to settle down in Linton."

"That's wonderful. I'm sure the local historical society will be devastated, but they didn't have enough money to buy this place, anyway, never mind finding the staff to keep it open on a regular basis. Did you know that Andrew Jackson came to tea at Bellefleur and that the explorer John Fremont slept in the guest room?" Velma waved her glass for emphasis. "Your aunt knew every detail of the history of this place, where every object in it came from, even when the wallpaper was hung. She was quite a character, your aunt."

Nickie nodded as Velma went on to explain the complicated feud that had gone on between her aunt and the Linton Historical Society for the past thirty years, touching on various amusing highlights of the confrontation. Nickie felt a pang of envy at the way Velma knew about everyone in town, their relationship to each other and the histories of their families; Nickie had never had roots before, but she assured herself she was going to start growing them now.

"Just give a holler if you think I'm getting too nosy or too personal, and I'll shut my mouth. At least for a while." Velma chuckled as she smoothed her skirt. "It's awful hard to resist someone who has secrets I don't already know all about. New blood ain't easy to come by in these parts."

Nickie grinned crookedly. "I can imagine."

"So, what do you do? For a living, I mean."

"I'm an illustrator."

"You mean drawing pictures for books?"

"Exactly. I've done several children's books, and right now I'm working on the illustrations for a guide to reptiles and amphibians."

"Ugh. Never did like slithery creatures, especially the kind that don't make any noise." She shuddered as she drained the last of her drink. "Never did like ghosts, either, although I can't say I ever personally met one. Marie-Claire always insisted she had, though."

Nickie's eyes widened and she sat straighter in her chair. "She did?"

"Yes, indeed. Right here in this house. That's why she threw me out, because I scoffed at her when she told me." Velma frowned and shook her head impatiently, although the movement did little to disturb her ironclad hairdo. "I don't suppose I should be filling your head with these fanciful old tales."

"Why not? That way I'll be prepared if I should ever bump into Bellefleur's resident ghost on the stairs." Nickie's eyes were shining as she leaned forward eagerly. "What kind of a spirit was it?"

"That's just it—I don't know. There I was, so busy snickering over the notion of a ghost in a quiet little town like Linton that I didn't even notice she was getting so fired up mad. She said only certain people could see it, anyway, and then she called me a commoner and tossed me out on my ear."

"Good heavens." Nickie grinned in amusement. "My aunt was always very proud of the family's connection to the Comte de Provence, but calling you a commoner—" she shook her head and laughed "—that's carrying matters to extremes."

"I thought she was kidding, but she never spoke to me again." Velma shrugged philosophically. "We weren't real chummy, anyway. As far as I know, she wasn't close to anybody in this town. Didn't think we were good enough to associate with, I suppose. I never heard anything more about the ghost after that. I just figured she'd been alone too much."

"I'm sure that's what it was," Nickie said soothingly. "Any house that has a lot of history connected with it usually has a ghost story, as well. After all, this place was built in the early 1800s."

Her visitor stood up. "Well, honey, I'm going to cut you a break and cart myself home. But don't you worry, I'll be back."

"Thank you for the soup, Mrs. Dare."

"It's Velma. And you're welcome. When you see Griff, you tell that wayward son of a gun that he'd better stop by and see me if he values his good name in this town."

"All right, I will."

She stood at the screen door and watched Velma march stolidly down the driveway until she disappeared around the corner where the gardener's cottage met the high walls of the main gate. Even though the gardener's residence had always been called a cottage, the structure had been built in the same style as the main house and was larger than most modern homes. A lovely screened-in porch extended beyond the front facade to provide both shade and architectural symmetry.

Nickie had already decided to go through the papers and books in the library on the second floor so she could learn more about the history of the estate;

now she had the more intriguing purpose of finding out if there were any ghost stories connected with the place. She had always been fascinated by such things, and since Bellefleur had become hers she discovered that her curiosity had accelerated from idle to avid. After all, this house and the people who'd lived in it were part of her heritage, a fact she'd never truly appreciated before.

She wondered briefly about Harry's grandson, Griffin McInnis, who had grown up to build bridges. She wondered what he looked like now; he'd been a big handsome boy of fifteen the one time she had met him. It was too bad he wasn't a gardener like his grandfather, who had worked for Marie-Claire for almost fifty years. She supposed that if her father hadn't been transferred to Maine when she was twelve, she might have had more encounters with the gardener's grandson, instead of just that one afternoon.

She wandered slowly upstairs, her hand caressing the polished oak railing with affection. Afternoon sunlight slanted across the papered walls, and she'd already learned that the fifth stair creaked if she stepped directly in the center of it. She felt gloriously happy, as though she knew the most wonderful secret in the world.

In an odd way she was reminded of the time when she'd had a best friend and they'd told each other everything about their lives, including their deepest thoughts and wildest dreams. She'd never forgotten the moment her father had announced they were moving again—she'd thought her heart would break from the wrenching pain of their separation. But she'd learned her lesson well, and never again had she opened up to someone who couldn't remain permanently in her life.

This time, however, she was here to stay, so there was no danger in opening her heart to Bellefleur. She breathed in the unique scent of the place. Even as a child she had been enchanted with the soft scented air inside the house, which always smelled as though someone had set out vases of freshly cut flowers. Maybe a house couldn't return your affection, but it could never cause you unhappiness, either.

She reached the interfloor landing. Marie-Claire's prized Louis XIV table still sat there, its dark wood gleaming softly in the filtered light. Nickie ran her hand across it reverently, her tactile sense delighting in the smooth polished finish. A faint scent of furniture wax lingered in the air. Her aunt had never wanted her to touch anything when she was a child, and at this moment she could almost sympathize with her protectiveness.

Nickie had never owned more than could be packed into the trunk of a car; even after she'd left home for good she discovered she'd become too used to her gypsy ways to stop moving from place to place. She realized now that she had always been looking for some perfect spot to call home. But none of the places she'd lived in spoke directly to her soul the way Bellefleur did. Now that she was here, she vowed to cherish the house and everything in it.

She had dusted and vacuumed and straightened in a frenzy of joyful possession the first two days after she'd arrived, and she swore she could feel the house coming alive under her ministrations. It was almost as though Marie-Claire had been the housekeeper, rather than the owner, but of course that was a conceited notion. She chuckled as she dropped her hand to her side; it was more likely that the ghost owned the house and they were all visitors here on sufferance.

The thought had barely cleared her brain when suddenly the hallway brightened. Nickie instinctively looked around to find out where the sunlight was coming from, but then realized there couldn't be any direct sunlight since this part of the hallway was between floors and had no windows. Yet, as she continued to gaze around, the space in front of her became even more illuminated. She frowned, puzzled.

Oddly enough she didn't feel frightened, even though "haunted" was the first word that flashed across her mind. This was her house and she loved it. She was sure no harm would come to her while she was safely within its walls. It must have been Velma with her silly talk of ghosts that had put her imagination into overdrive.

The light continued to grow brighter, only now it seemed to be beckoning her from the far end of the corridor, just above and around the corner from the study where she had been working all morning. It was almost as though someone had a Coleman lamp just out of sight; the light was too diffuse and glowing to come from a flashlight and too concentrated to be sunlight.

"Hello. Is someone there?" she called out softly.

She felt foolish as soon as the words left her mouth. Of course nobody answered her. She would have jumped a mile if they had. By now, however, she was beginning to grow concerned and more than a little nervous. She quickly reminded herself that she hadn't eaten any breakfast; she had awakened first thing that morning with a full-blown idea for the lizard sketch and had rushed across to the study, the one with the Dresden Owl lamp that had so fascinated her as a child, where she had buckled right down to work. She could be light-headed from lack of food.

Maybe now was as good a time as any to go back downstairs and have something to eat, she quickly decided. Maybe she would even step outside and stroll through the gardens again, get some fresh air. Her chest felt tight and constricted, and she was having trouble breathing because her heart was pumping so hard.

As this jumble of thoughts whirled through her mind, she suddenly noticed that the noisy chatter of the birds had stopped. She cocked her head to listen, but it was as though she were inside a vacuum because she couldn't seem to hear any noise at all.

Although she didn't want to, she found herself swallowing hard and lifting her gaze to check out the mysterious light one more time. Now it looked more like a roiling mass of light and particles. The entire thing swirled like some kind of giant dust mote gone mad or like one of those dust devils whirling down a dirt road she'd often seen as a child in summer. Could a dust devil form inside a house? Had the place been closed up so long while Aunt Marie-Claire's will had been sorted out that the dust had taken over in this odd fashion?

The hair at the nape of her neck began to rise even as she felt a small spark of annoyance. Darn it all, she assured herself vigorously, this was *her* house. It belonged to her as surely as she had always felt its stable presence in her life all these years. She didn't want anything to spoil that bond, certainly not this freakish physical phenomenon that had appeared out of nowhere to disturb her quiet afternoon.

She blinked, but it was still there, curling and shifting and moving in her direction. She automatically thrust out her hand, giving a good imitation of a traffic cop halting a line of traffic. As if a ball of dust obeyed hand signals. She wasn't surprised when it continued to swirl.

She knew she should move, but she couldn't seem to pull her attention away from the shimmering spectacle. If she wasn't careful she would find herself mesmerized into a trance right here in the hallway. There was something inherently fascinating about the way the particles floated and danced as they reflected the mysterious light that seemed to be coming from everywhere and nowhere at once.

She realized she was still holding her hand out and allowed it to drop limply to her side. As if that was a signal, the cloud of dust suddenly shifted direction. Her relief that it had stopped moving toward her was short-lived. She watched in growing horror as the shapeless sprawling mass began condensing itself in a vertical direction, growing taller as it gathered form and dimension until it almost looked like—

"No!" she heard herself protesting.

But at least the sight had shocked her into action. She turned and sprinted down the stairs and out the front door.

## Chapter Two

Griff McInnis hefted his small overnight bag, gripping it more firmly in his hand as he continued walking along the road toward Bellefleur. Dappled sunlight filtered through the line of trees, which provided a tunnel of cool shade, and the soft balmy air that pressed against him was thick with the scent of newly cut grass. Memories of the summers he had spent here as a boy came flooding back with a sharpness that surprised him. He even remembered to watch out for the notorious rise in the sidewalk where it had cracked and buckled over the massive roots of the Wilsons' old pecan tree.

At the corner of Second and Main he cut diagonally across the street. The heat of the southern sun felt good on the top of his head after so many months in Buffalo. He quickly decided he wouldn't even think about his next project. The bridge he'd been hired to repair in Southern California could wait; now he needed to concentrate on the task he'd set for himself here in Linton. His grandfather's peace of mind was more important than any number of bridges.

He would know better how to proceed after he saw the new owner of Bellefleur. It might be a bit tricky with only ten days in which to accomplish the job, but he couldn't imagine that Nickie DuPrés would be averse to accepting his offer. She'd probably jump at the chance.

He'd only met her once, but the impression remained of a self-possessed little girl who had tagged along behind him at a respectful distance for most of a summer afternoon. Every time he'd turned around she'd busied herself with the lumpy-looking doll that never left her possession. Of course, he had been a swaggering fifteen-year-old while she'd been just a skinny little kid of ten or eleven. He hadn't been able to decide whether she was just shy and withdrawn, or if she was trying to follow in the footsteps of her snooty great-aunt who would never have condescended to hobnob with the hired help.

His pace slowed as he approached the next intersection. He knew the exact location from which to catch his first glimpse of Bellefleur's gardens. Even from this distance the sight of the magnificent statue of Apollo made him catch his breath. The Greek god, draped in robes that artfully concealed his masculine charms, stood shaded by a brace of silver maples as his muscular yet graceful arm indicated the way to Neptune's Fountain.

His grandfather had certainly created a masterpiece. In fact, he had spent a good portion of his adult life making Bellefleur's gardens one of the great showplaces of the South. He'd been truly happy doing so, although Griff still felt his grandfather had been shortchanged. The pronounced limp that remained from an injury he'd received in World War II had never hindered Harry McInnis, never impaired his inherent skills and abilities, but he was so grateful to Marie-Claire DuPrés for taking him on as gardener that he never protested her superior attitude toward him. Griff had eventually come to realize that she treated everyone that way. Nevertheless, he still bristled over her attitude.

He wondered how bad things really were on the estate. Without his granddad there to care for the place he imagined it was pretty overgrown. According to his sister Tracy, the lawn and gardens had fallen into serious disrepair this past year. It saddened him to think that something his grandfather had cared for so passionately and with such painstaking devotion was dying. No wonder the sight of Bellefleur in its current unkempt state had sent the old man into a tailspin, so much so that Harry still hadn't completely recovered.

Griff couldn't restrain the lump in his throat when he caught his first glimpse of the cottage, sitting inside the main gate. It looked the same as always, with its white shingles glistening in the sunlight and its black awnings providing a tasteful counterpart. The hedges around the front porch were taller than he remembered, and as he got closer he could see they hadn't been trimmed in some time; as a result, the place had an abandoned appearance, and even though he'd been prepared for it, he still felt faintly shocked. After the fastidiousness of his grandfather's reign over every aspect of the grounds, this was a tragedy indeed.

Griff tossed his bag onto the porch before continuing up the driveway to the main house. Marie-Claire's grandniece had parked her small car off to one side, and he could see that the front door of the main house was open. Although Dutch had given him the key to the cottage, he didn't want to take the time to open up the place. The sooner he saw Dominique DuPrés, the sooner he'd be able to assess her grown-up character and figure out which tactic would get him what he wanted.

He only hoped he wouldn't have to charm her; he wasn't a naturally charming kind of guy. He couldn't see the need to beat around the bush with small talk when he could get right to the point. Most people considered his attitude blunt if honest, but some women found it hard to take when it came to relationships. He wondered how the aristocratic Ms. DuPrés would handle him.

Gravel crunched under his feet and the sound of birds filled the air. He'd always associated Bellefleur with birds, but he couldn't remember anything like the raucous din that now filled his ears. It seemed to be coming from the back of the house where the old arbor used to be. Maybe a squirrel had invaded their territory, he thought, but then decided against the idea. These birds weren't crying out in alarm, they were chirping in a normal everyday fashion. It was just that there seemed to be so many of them.

He had almost reached the bottom of the wooden porch stairs when he heard the sound of pounding feet, and then a woman burst through the screen door. She was looking back over her shoulder at the house, and he barely had time to register that she was clad in threadbare jeans and a soft yellow T-shirt before she flung herself into him.

He caught her before she could knock them both to the ground. Her startled eyes flew to meet his as she automatically grasped his forearm with both hands for balance. Her skin seemed unnaturally cool. Maybe it was just that his own flesh was heated from the long walk.

"You're holding me, you know," he said, smiling. He knew he sounded friendly and casual. It wasn't the easiest attitude to maintain especially when the rapid rise and fall of her chest kept bringing her T-shirt-covered breasts within millimeters of his knuckles. "Not that I mind," he added truthfully.

She turned to look at him. "Griff," she said with an answering smile, her voice strained and slightly breathless. She pulled in a lungful of air before releasing his arm with a sheepish lift of her eyebrows. She quickly dropped her hands to her sides.

He allowed himself to study her. She was small and fine-boned, although her hair was darker than he remembered and curled around her face most engagingly. She certainly hadn't grown up to resemble her dragon of an aunt. Her eyes were wide, almost beseeching, and their color matched her hair.

"Just give me a minute to catch my breath," she said.

"No problem."

He looked up at the screen door, half expecting to see someone come crashing out behind her, but the house was still. He glanced down at her slender hands, which were now clutched at her waist. Her skin looked smooth and soft, and so pale it reminded him of marble, especially since he already knew her hands were as cool as a piece of sculpture.

When she still didn't speak he decided to try a more active approach. "What happened? Did something frighten you?"

"No, of course not." She eased her hands apart and politely smiled up at him as though she hadn't just come barreling down the porch stairs like the hounds of hell were on her tail. He found himself admiring her suddenly acquired poise and battling an untoward urge to reach out and touch her.

"I…I'm just not used to being in the country where it's so quiet." She offered the explanation with a self-deprecating little smile. "Every old house has its share of creaks and groans, I suppose, but I've never lived in one before. Sounds seem to be magnified all out of proportion."

"You mean like the racket those birds in the back-yard are making."

"The birds?" She looked lost for a moment, then she exclaimed in a rush, "Oh, yes, those birds. I hear them now! They are rather loud, aren't they?"

Her relief was palpable and suspiciously out of proportion, given the content of his casual observation. Griff eyed her thoughtfully, wondering what was going on. This woman wasn't telling him the entire truth about what had happened in the house. Perhaps she'd received an upsetting phone call from a boy-friend, although why that should frighten her he had no idea. In any case, he didn't figure it was any of his business.

"I guess Dutch told you I'd be arriving today."

"Dutch?" Even though her gaze met his, she still seemed distracted, her brow wrinkled in puzzlement.

"Harold Cohen, the lawyer here in town."

"Oh, yes. Yes, he told me. He said you wanted to look for some books of your grandfather's."

Her dark eyes and pale skin were truly lovely. Griff had to remind himself not to stare. "I don't think it'll take very long," he said. "I figured I'd stay in the cottage for a few days, if that's all right with you."

"Yes, of course. My aunt made it quite clear in her will that your grandfather could stay on in the cottage for as long as he wanted. In fact, I expected to find him there when I arrived."

"Yeah, well, he had a small stroke last year and had to go live with my sister in Memphis. The grounds of Bellefleur meant everything to him, and he didn't want to stay on if he wasn't physically capable of looking after things."

"Yes, I can imagine that would be hard on him after creating something so wonderful." Her graceful gesture took in the back of the house where the gardens lay.

They both fell silent. Griff thought about opening another line of conversation and then decided it wouldn't make a bit of difference to the outcome of his request. She seemed friendly enough; she certainly didn't come across haughty and demanding like Marie-Claire. But then, he wasn't working for her. Nor did he intend to, he assured himself. He might as well get on with it.

"I have a favor to ask." He deliberately met her eyes so she could see for herself that he wasn't trying to hand her a line. "It concerns my grandfather."

"What is it?"

"I . . . This is going to sound strange, but I want to clean up the gardens—you know, mow the lawns, trim the hedges, weed the flower beds. It wouldn't take much to spruce everything up and have it looking the way it used to."

"Good heavens, why would you want to do that?"

He shrugged, his smile crooked. "So I can bring my grandfather here. So he can see that the legacy he left is being cared for the way it should be."

"Are you implying I'm to blame for this neglect?" Her voice held a hint of indignation. "I only just got here, but I assure you I have every intention of hiring another gardener."

"Yes, but that might take you a while, and time is of the essence here, since I only have a couple of weeks until I have to be in California." His mouth tightened. "Granddad hasn't been well since my sister made the mistake of taking him for a drive past the grounds several weeks ago."

"Oh, I see." Nickie bit her lip. "You think that if your grandfather saw that things were back to normal he would feel better?"

"It certainly wouldn't hurt. According to his doctor, he's depressed." Which was true enough, Griff supposed, as far as it went. He wasn't about to tell Nickie DuPrés the real reason behind his desire to whip the gardens back into shape. She might think he was crazy.

"That's very nice of you, but I couldn't allow you to do all that work for nothing," she said earnestly, gazing up at him. "I'd like to pay you. Aunt Marie-Claire set aside money for a gardener, although it isn't the greatest sum in the world."

"No, no, I don't want any money," he quickly protested. The thought of finding himself embroiled in

the same kind of lady-of-the-manor/gardener relationship his grandfather had endured with Marie-
Claire made him shudder. "You'd be doing me a favor by allowing me to help my grandfather."

"Some favor," she replied. Her entire face came
alive when she grinned like that. "Okay, why not."

"Great. Thanks." He hadn't really believed she
would refuse, but his relief was tremendous all the
same. He wondered if she had any suspicions about his
request.

"This is wonderful," she continued, her brown eyes
sparkling with excitement. "I can't wait to see the
gardens in their full glory. Up until now I've only seen
pictures."

"You mean you've never been in these gardens before?"

"Not until the other day," she replied with a small
shrug and a faintly guilt-ridden smile. "We were never
a very close-knit family. I only visited my aunt a couple of times as a child. That time I met you was the last
time I ever saw her, which is why it was such a shock
when her lawyer told me I had inherited Bellefleur."

"I can imagine," he replied politely. He watched her
gaze around the front yard, a dreamy expression on
her face. She reminded him of a dancer, all sleek
curves and controlled graceful motion.

"I suppose I don't know much about it, but even in
their current condition, the grounds still look beautiful to me." She turned toward him and her eyes were
luminous. "I've never seen so many colorful flowers,
and I love those sculpted bushes, even if they are a bit
overgrown. And then there's the fountain with that
impressive statue of Neptune in it." She shook her

head. "I wanted to turn it on, but I had no idea where to find the switch."

"I'll look for it first thing tomorrow."

"Oh, would you? Thanks. I'm shamefully ignorant about so many aspects of this place. I'm hoping some of those books in the library will help me."

"Did you know that your great-aunt wanted everything to resemble the gardens at Versailles, the way they were before the French Revolution? On a more modest scale, of course."

She laughed in pleased surprise. "I knew they were magnificent, but I never realized they were modeled on Versailles. I should have suspected, though, knowing my great-aunt's unquestioned devotion to anything connected with French royalty."

Griff nodded in reply, but he was puzzled. It was hard to believe Nickie knew so little about Bellefleur's gardens. According to his grandfather, Marie-Claire DuPrés had made no secret of the fact that she intended to leave the entire estate to her grandniece. He couldn't imagine the haughty old woman doing so without grooming Nickie to follow in her precise aristocratic footsteps.

"My grandfather had to research Louis XVI and Marie Antoinette," he informed her, more to cover his thoughts than to give her a history lesson. He was trying his best to consider her dispassionately, but he found himself distracted by the pure clarity of her face with its fine-boned elegance and porcelain complexion. And although he didn't believe in a class system or hold with the notion that some people were inherently better than others merely by virtue of their bloodlines, he was damned if she didn't look like some well-bred aristocrat whose hands had never been soiled with work and whose mind had never been faced with the coarse realities of everyday life.

"Marie-Claire even sent him over to Paris so he could see for himself the actual size and layout of the palace gardens," he added.

She sighed wistfully. "I wish someone would send me over to Paris for some firsthand experience."

"She told him she only wanted him to plant the kinds of flowers and shrubbery that grew in that part of France."

"Good heavens," Nickie said, her face expressing amazement tinged with fond exasperation. "I can't say I'm surprised. She loved everything French, especially if it had to do with the Bourbon kings. But that's certainly taking a whim beyond the point of casual interest, don't you think?"

"I can't believe you don't know about all this already," he said, trying not to sound accusing.

She shook her head as she allowed her sparkling gaze to meet his. He felt his insides tighten in an unwanted but instinctive reaction to the softly feminine appeal of her warm smile. What a combination of reactions she was calling forth from him, he thought in mild exasperation. He certainly hadn't expected that skinny little girl to turn out anything like this beautiful young woman.

He had no desire to experience this sensual pull in her direction, not when he wouldn't be around long enough to make anything come of it. Also, in spite of his generally egalitarian fix on life, he wasn't completely comfortable entertaining thoughts of too much intimacy with this particular woman. For one thing,

she now owned a historically priceless estate bequeathed to her by the French blue blood of all time.
For another, his grandfather used to work for her
great-aunt. Along with the usual and inevitable male-
female misunderstandings that were bound to arise, it
added up to more excess baggage than he cared to
handle.

"It sounds like you know a lot about this place,"
she said, again with that wistful expression she seemed
to get on her face when she spoke of Bellefleur's history. She straightened her shoulders. "Well, I will,
too, very soon."

"I'd better go get settled in." He held up the key to
the cottage, forcing his features into a polite smile.

"That's fine. If you need anything, just let me
know." She smiled at him before turning toward the
house.

Griff watched her go, wondering what she would
think if she knew the real reason behind his desire to
tend to the gardens. He hadn't told any outright lies
about his grandfather's condition—Harry *had* become quite agitated over the state of Bellefleur's
grounds. And Griff supposed that the doctor's diagnosis of clinical depression was as good a label as any
to apply to the old man's precarious state of mental
and physical health.

But how could Griff even begin to explain that his
grandfather wasn't upset about the gardens for his
own sake, that he wasn't concerned about the loss of
all his fine efforts to future generations. No, sir. Every
time Griff closed his eyes he could almost feel Harry
grasping his arm with strong fingers, his eyes glinting
wildly as he begged his grandson to hurry and refur-

bish the gardens because the ghost of Bellefleur wished
it.

AFTER HER SOLITARY DINNER, Nickie pushed open the
screen door and went out to stand on the front porch.
It was a beautiful late-spring evening, although now
that the sun was below the horizon the air had acquired enough of a chill to make her wish she'd put on
a sweater. She crossed her arms over her chest for
warmth and gazed around the once neatly manicured
yard. Although the estate lawyer had sent someone out
to mow the lawn, the shrubbery remained overgrown.

She had always loved the spacious layout and elegant proportions of the circular gravel driveway, which
swept past the front door. It soothed her modern-day
psyche in ways she couldn't begin to express. A marble birdbath added a touch of whimsy to the grassy
sloping lawn. Of course, all this had been designed for
an earlier, more graceful age when horse-drawn car-
riages had rumbled to a stop at the main entrance to
Bellefleur, and elegantly dressed ladies had disem-
barked to sweep up the grand front steps.

Her gaze drifted to the cottage, and she realized why
she was feeling so restless and out of sorts, and why
she'd been lured outside, away from the texts she'd
been perusing in preparation for tomorrow's work. A
rueful smile crossed her features as she wondered what
Griff was doing. She was sure he wasn't hanging
around the cottage wondering the same thing about
her. The man had come here with a purpose, and he
didn't look like the sort to linger over a cup of coffee,
never mind a task he had set for himself.

She had to admit she'd been hard hit by the impact of the handsome Griff McInnis. Common sense told her that the time to come to terms with her incipient infatuation was right now, when it could be handled quickly and decisively. She assured herself it shouldn't be all that difficult under the circumstances, not when the man was only going to be here a short time.

She noticed a light on in one of the second-floor windows of the gardener's cottage, which was why she was startled when the object of her thoughts stepped out the front door, almost as if he'd been waiting for her to appear. What a nonsensical notion! she thought. In spite of her best intentions, she couldn't stop herself from raising her arm in a friendly wave.

To her pleased surprise, he started down the porch steps and began walking toward her. Deep inside, an oddly atavistic instinct urged her to turn and run, but she ignored it in favor of studying him as he approached, walking with that compact stride of his she'd noted earlier. It seemed made to conserve energy for things that really mattered.

She estimated that he was about six feet tall, of medium build, which fell just short of being stocky, with a head of thick black hair. He was clean-shaven with well-defined features and a broad forehead that suggested stubbornness to her artist's eye. Maybe it was the combination of the name McInnis and her vivid imagination, but Nickie decided he wouldn't look out of place wearing a fisherman's sweater and skulking around a pub somewhere in Ireland—he had that same look of toughness, like a man who knew how to use his fists to good effect in a back alley. But it was his eyes that moved him into a category beyond average: they were as green as the finest emeralds and framed with dark lashes. When they gazed at her they seemed to cut through her like laser beams.

"Good evening," he said as soon as he was close enough to speak without raising his voice. He had on jeans and a dark work shirt with the sleeves pushed back to his elbows. He looked vital and alive, even in the rapidly dimming light. She swore she could actually feel the vibrations coming from his body, as though he couldn't help generating an overabundance of unprocessed masculine energy. "I was hoping you would take me on a guided tour of the gardens before it got completely dark."

As she leaned on the porch railing above him, she had the oddest impression that he had come out here against his will, although she couldn't imagine him doing anything he didn't want. Her heart jerked in response to the inherent promise of the moment by slamming against her chest for a startled beat before kicking into an accelerated rhythm that forced her to take deeper breaths. The awareness suddenly thrumming between them was almost palpable in the still night air, like electricity running along a high-tension wire.

"Okay," she agreed quietly. "I have to warn you that I don't know my way around all that well, and it'll probably be pitch-dark in another ten minutes or so. I can't promise we won't end up in the fountain."

He chuckled softly and the sound sent a shiver up her spine. "How about if we just follow this pathway around the house? That should be safe enough." His eyes continued to glint sporadically in the rapidly fading twilight, although they now looked black and fathomless, rather than green.

"All right."

She couldn't deny that she wanted to be with him, that she was drawn to him like a hapless moth to a flame. Maybe it was the fault of the glorious full moon that rode high in the sky, but it seemed that fate was offering her a magical moment out of time. She would be a fool not to take it.

Gravel crunched beneath their feet as they strolled along the path that led to the entrance of the main gardens around back. Nickie was terribly aware of Griff walking along beside her with that easy, almost rocking motion of his as he matched his longer strides to hers. She peered at him surreptitiously through the curtain of her lashes, certain he couldn't tell what she was doing in the distorting moonlight that filtered through the trees. Then it occurred to her that he might be aware of her glance, in spite of her precautions, in the same way she was attuned to the faint tension in his body. The effect of this almost supernatural awareness she had suddenly acquired of him was both uncomfortable and exhilarating.

"I almost forgot to tell you that Velma Dare wants you to stop by," she commented as they rounded the corner of the house and moved into the darker shadows of the backyard.

"Thanks for the message. I've already seen her."

"Oh."

"After she got finished lecturing me about my prodigal ways, she told me a few things about you."

Nickie grinned. "No kidding."

"She mentioned that you're an illustrator."

"That's right. At the moment I'm working on a book about lizards and other scaly creatures." She smiled. This was a topic that felt safe, and she grasped at it as gratefully as someone drowning grasps at a life preserver. "My publisher moved me up the evolutionary scale to reptiles after my book on insects and spiders made the national children's-books bestseller list. Hopefully, after I finish the last section on snakes, I'll be able to move on to birds."

"You'll have enough real-life models to work from around here."

"You said it." She chuckled. "It's odd, isn't it, that so many birds congregate in this one particular spot. I wonder what attracts them?"

She glanced up toward the large elm tree, and as she did, she saw a light flash as something moved behind one of the second-floor windows of the house. She drew a startled breath.

"What is it?" he asked.

She looked up and there it was again, very faint but definitely there. "Look, that window on the second floor," she said breathlessly, pointing. "Can you see something moving? And a light?"

He stared at her for a long intense moment before turning his gaze toward the window. "I don't see anything. Maybe you forgot to turn off the lights."

"I'm sure I didn't." She bit her lip in consternation as her mind replayed her actions before she'd come downstairs to make dinner. She was positive she'd switched everything off. She remembered it so distinctly because at the time she'd been worrying about the size of her future electricity bill. "I suppose there could be a faulty connection in the wiring somewhere. Or perhaps it's Velma's ghost," she added jokingly.

"Velma's ghost?" His sharp tone startled her.

"Sure. Though it's not actually Velma's." She glanced over at him as she explained, "She told me this afternoon that my aunt claimed to have seen a ghost on the premises."

"And now you're seeing one, too."

"Hey, wait a minute," she protested, her tone mildly amused. "I didn't say I saw a ghost—just movement in the window. It was probably only a reflection." She pressed her lips together thoughtfully, wondering if she should mention the dust cloud. She was more than a little curious to see what kind of a reaction that would elicit. "Although now that we're on the subject, something odd happened earlier."

"What was that?" he asked politely.

His words sounded forced as though he had no desire to hear what Nickie had to say, but she told him, anyway. "Well, don't laugh, but I saw an odd swirling cloud of dust in the upstairs hallway."

She watched him as carefully as she could in the shadowy darkness. She didn't have high expectations that the serious Griff would believe her unsubstantiated tale of runaway dust just because she said it was so, although a part of her wistfully wished he would. Just because she'd seen the darn thing with her own eyes didn't make it sound any less crazy.

"Is that why you came tearing out of the house?"

She nodded, then realized he might not be able to see her in the dark. "Yes."

"A swirling cloud of dust," he repeated neutrally. "Sounds like the place could use a thorough cleaning."

Although she could detect the faintest trace of humorous disbelief threading through his voice, something else was there, as well, almost as though he'd been expecting something like this and hoping against hope not to find it.

She frowned in mild exasperation. She'd been right about his response, not that it gave her any satisfaction. "I know I'm not the greatest housekeeper in the world, but I did dust and vacuum the day after I arrived."

"Maybe you missed a spot."

"Very funny. I take it you don't believe in anything supernatural?"

"No."

"It does sound pretty ludicrous, doesn't it?" She found herself wanting to shrug away the incident under Griff's probing scrutiny. "I'm sure you're right. My imagination must have been working overtime." She turned to face him. "I suppose I've always felt this house was enchanted. It must have something to do with the strange man I saw standing in that very same window when I was a child."

"Was he a ghost?"

She made a face at him. "I don't know. He wasn't wearing a sign that said Ghost, and I never got the chance to ask him. He certainly looked real enough to me. And when I waved to him, he waved back." She smiled in fond remembrance. "My aunt wouldn't tell me who he was, but when I got older I figured she had a secret lover she didn't want anyone to know about."

Griff's reaction was a snort.

"Are you implying that my esteemed aunt was a basically unlovable woman?" she asked with an amused chuckle.

He grinned back, his white teeth glinting in the moonlight. "I wouldn't dream of it."

"I guess she made it pretty difficult for people to like her. To be quite honest, *I* had a hard time liking her. She was sharp-tempered and overly proud and consumed to the point of obsession with Bellefleur." She sighed as she plucked a leaf from a nearby tree and began toying with it. "I never thought she liked me much, either."

"Then why'd she leave this place to you?"

"I don't know. Maybe she had no one else to leave it to. Or maybe she sensed how much I loved Bellefleur."

Griff leaned his shoulder casually against one of the smaller maple trees that grew alongside the walkway, sliding his hands into his pockets. "My grandfather was one of those Irishmen who believed in leprechauns and banshees and things that go bump in the night," he said casually.

"Did he really? Did he ever mention anything about a ghost in connection with Bellefleur?"

A shaft of moonlight illuminated Griff's face as he stared at her with narrowed speculative eyes. She could see he'd brought the subject up on purpose, just so she would ask that exact question.

"As a matter of fact, he did mention it once or twice," he finally answered with slow deliberation. "One evening Marie-Claire took him into the garden and pointed out a mysterious something in the window, just like you did a minute ago. Don't you find that an odd coincidence?''

"Not if there was something in the window," she retorted, carelessly tossing the crumpled leaf to the ground. She didn't like where this conversation seemed to be headed. "What are you implying?''

"Nothing." He straightened away from the tree. "Come on, it's getting dark. We'd better head back." He motioned for her to precede him, but she remained stubbornly by the hedge.

"Just a minute, Griff."

He immediately dropped his hand. So much for her secret hopes for a romantic stroll in the moonlight, she thought wryly. "Before you disappear in a puff of smoke, let me ask you something." She shook her head to toss a wayward strand of hair from her eyes and stepped into the center of the pathway. "Are you saying there's a purpose behind all this? That I'm trying to trick you into thinking you're seeing a ghost?''

"It was just a passing theory. It doesn't make any sense now that I think about it, so please just forget I brought it up." He turned and began walking away from her. This time she trotted along behind him.

"Why would I want you to see a ghost?''

"Drop it, Nickie."

"Did your grandfather ever see a ghost?''

He stopped walking so abruptly she almost ran into him. "He never actually saw the ghost, but he believed in it," he admitted reluctantly.

"Are you talking about the ghost of Bellefleur?'' she whispered in awe. "You mean there really is one?''

He whirled around to confront her. "Hang on a minute," he said, blowing out an exasperated breath.

"I never said that Bellefleur had a ghost. There's never been a shred of evidence to prove it, although that never seems to stop anyone."

"You mean my aunt?"

"For one."

"Then why does your grandfather also believe in the ghost if he never saw it?"

"I don't know." He sounded annoyed, but his touch was gentle as he reached out to grasp her by the elbow and urge her forward. The heel of his shoe sent a piece of gravel skittering across the path as they rounded the corner at the front of the house. "The one thing I do know is that the best way to help him recover completely is by restoring the gardens, and that's what I intend to do."

He dropped her arm and they continued the short distance to the driveway in silence, although strangely enough, it wasn't an uncomfortable one. Nickie's mind raced as she considered Griff's astounding revelation that another person besides her aunt actually believed in the ghost of Bellefleur. If she included Velma in her calculations, that meant the tally was two votes for the ghost and two against. Did that mean she held the tiebreaking vote?

She smiled crookedly as she glanced over at Griff. His unwillingness to speculate about Bellefleur's ghost didn't dampen her appreciation of his being by her side on this beautiful balmy night. She breathed in the pungent smell of wet grass and shrubbery that permeated the air.

He halted at the edge of the pool of light that spilled from the corner window. "Thanks for the tour."

"We didn't get to see very much."

"I wouldn't say that. Good night, Nickie." Without another word he strode across the lawn where it dipped past the birdbath and continued toward the cottage. She could actually see traces of his damp footprints glistening in the moonlight.

Nickie watched him disappear inside, her brows raised in droll amusement at this abrupt conclusion to the evening stroll in the gardens.

"Good night, Griff," she said. She smiled as she slowly climbed the porch stairs, dragging her hand along behind her on the railing. Her smile broadened to a grin.

Things were certainly getting interesting around here.

## Chapter Three

Griff let the front door bang closed behind him as he stepped into the cottage. His adrenaline was still quietly flowing, both from his walk with Nickie and from the encounter with his worst nightmare come true—the return of the supposed ghost of Bellefleur. He couldn't believe he'd only been back several hours and already the debate was raging.

He snorted in disgust as he stalked through the living room into the kitchen. He supposed that once a house got a reputation for any kind of supernatural phenomenon, the thing became a juggernaut, almost impossible to stop. Of course this was no ordinary ghost who haunted stairwells in the respectable, time-honored manner of other spooks and spirits. Oh, no, according to Marie-Claire DuPrés, this ghost had to have a garden paradise to showcase his talents.

He still couldn't believe that his grandfather had bought into Marie-Claire's grandiose scheme, in spite of the spectacular results. Harry McInnis had always been too Gaelic for his own good, and the thought of building a garden for a ghost must have tickled his Irish fancy. Griff grimaced as he recalled how wan his grandfather had appeared only a couple of days ago. He'd been as pale as his pillow. And the way he had pleaded with Griff to restore the gardens still made his throat tighten in helpless dismay. And all because of the wishes of a nonexistent ghost.

According to the doctor the old man was currently in the manic stage of a serious clinical depression. Griff didn't care about the diagnosis; he just wanted Harry out of that damned bed and back on his feet. In spite of his protests to the contrary, Harry Patrick McInnis was a proud man, and the monument to his determination to get the job done was still visible right outside this very door. Griff intended to keep it that way.

He still felt a surge of annoyance when he thought about Nickie excitedly reporting seeing a glimmer of light in that upstairs window. Although she'd later admitted it was most likely a reflection, she had forced him to bring the subject of the ghost into the open, and now there was probably no stopping the eventual repercussions.

Better to turn his mind to planning the task at hand, he thought as he paced the kitchen floor. Starting tomorrow, he would get the fountain running, then begin to trim back some of the plants and hedges. He knew it wouldn't take any great skill to return them to their full glory after their many years of diligent care, just patience and a week or so of backbreaking labor.

He reached into the refrigerator for one of the beers from the six-pack he had purchased earlier that afternoon. He might be able to stretch his vacation another day or two if necessary, but a maximum of two weeks was all the time he had to spruce up the place and bring his grandfather back for a visit.

As he popped the top he wondered what else could possibly go wrong.

NICKIE TRIED not to think of the swirling dust cloud as she climbed the stairs to the second floor. All this talk about ghosts had made her nervous, especially since it wasn't theoretical but applied specifically to the ghost of Bellefleur. She had taken over the master bedroom since it was the only room that had a decent bed, but it was located at the back of the house, and to get there she had to go through the hallway.

She assured herself that there was no light and therefore no illuminated dust. She had never been the kind of person who spooked easily, but she was discovering that being alone in the country was very different from being alone in the city. You might have to watch out for muggers and thieves in Boston, but you didn't have to worry about swirling dust and unexplained lights in an empty room. She giggled a bit hysterically because it all sounded so foolish, and then jumped at the sound of her own voice. She was just being silly, she decided, as she urged her feet forward.

It was the hardest thing she'd ever done. Her heart was racing and her skin felt clammy. She'd never been particularly susceptible to horror movies, but she found herself imagining all sorts of terrible things as she tiptoed quietly on the worn carpeting, as though she could sneak past, as though the huge dust mote was sleeping.

It was when she turned the corner at the top of the stairs that she saw him, just outside the doorway to her study. For a moment she thought she was imagining things. Then she feared she might faint, but the pounding of her heart was so loud, it kept her upright and immobile, her muscles frozen in a pose of startled surprise. She tried to tear her gaze away, but it was impossible not to look at the apparition that stood directly in her path. In any case, the cool sensible part of her brain insisted it might be better to watch him in case he started moving in her direction.

It was a ghost all right. She could see him and yet she could also see right through him to the doorway behind. He was dressed in nineteenth-century garb, maybe even eighteenth. She wasn't all that knowledgeable about men's fashions from those times, but he had on a double-breasted jacket that was cut away in the front and had long tails in the back. Underneath he wore a striped vest over a white shirt with ruffles at the throat and cuffs. His trousers were tight, fitting the contours of his long legs with loving smoothness, and they were tucked into soft-looking midcalf leather boots.

Even from this distance she could tell he was tall, because the top of his head was level with one of the small lamps that graced alternating sides of the walls and illuminated the hallway. In spite of her terror, she couldn't help but notice how handsome he was. He had dark hair that swept back from his brow and looked as though it might be tied at the nape of his neck. His forehead was broad and his features even and refined, like an aristocratic prince in a story.

He looked familiar. As she tried to overcome the waves of fear that beat harder and harder against the wall of her consciousness, she realized he resembled the man she had seen in the window of Bellefleur when she was a child. She couldn't be sure, of course; that had happened a long time ago and at a considerable distance. And yet something about the elegant way he carried himself struck an insistent note of familiarity.

The thought of that incident, and the sad longing that always accompanied the image of the man in the window, had a soothing effect on her. Not that she intended to take her eyes from whatever was standing in front of her now. She swallowed hard as the hysterical part of her brain continued to urge her to flee. She even found herself wishing for the return of the dust cloud as she remained rooted to the floor.

Of course, he didn't look as though he wanted to harm her in any way, but who could tell with a ghost? Just the fact that he was lurking around the hallways of Bellefleur, the home where she had decided to settle permanently, was a dismaying prospect—even if he did look as elegant as a peacock.

And then he moved. He gazed at her beseechingly as he extended his arm toward her. Then he lifted his other arm and pointed with ghostly vigor at the door to her study. What on earth did he want? she wondered frantically. She could see his mouth moving, but of course no sounds came out, and that made it even more horrifying.

Nickie swallowed hard, her throat muscles working convulsively as she tried not to scream. After all, when did screaming ever frighten a ghost? She also had to concentrate on not crumpling into a dead faint on the floor, or hyperventilating. She had the sinking feeling that her body was trying to achieve both those reactions at once, which helped to explain why she just stood frozen to the spot like a pillar of ice at the North Pole, instead of running away like any sensible person. Even the tiny muscles around her eyes refused to cooperate when she tried to blink the apparition away; all she could do was stare at him with such intense concentration it was almost painful.

He might look harmless, but it wasn't the easiest thing in the world to stand practically toe-to-toe with a ghost no matter how friendly he looked. She wasn't sure what changed, but suddenly something shifted inside her brain and she knew she couldn't stay there another second. Her circuits were overloaded and could handle no more.

"Hey, nice meeting you," she murmured politely as she began backing carefully toward the stairs. "See you around."

If she hadn't been so rattled, she would have laughed out loud at her efforts to maintain a veneer of politeness in the presence of an uninvited specter. She only hoped the ghost would appreciate the stress she was operating under, and not construe her words as an invitation to pay her a return visit.

He didn't seem inclined to do much of anything, including glide after her. He just stood there with a sadly resigned expression on his handsome face and lowered his hands to his sides. She continued to inch her way down the stairs, clutching the banister with sweaty palms while he stared at her halting progress from the landing above.

When she judged she was far enough away to risk it, she managed a small smile in his direction and headed for the screen door that led out into the cool night air. She couldn't help herself—he seemed so forlorn. Even though she was chilled to the marrow, she didn't mind the dampness that now surrounded and caressed the exposed skin of her face and arms. With a stifled sob of relief, she began running toward the cottage, the soles of her sneakers crunching on the gravel driveway. That homely sound was a welcome invitation back to reality, although the sight of her own shadow cast by the full moon startled her.

Without losing a step, she continued jogging across the lawn, her feet barely skimming the ground and her heartbeat again accelerating like the engine of a race car at the starting line.

GRIFF WAS ALREADY in bed, although still awake, when he heard the knocking at his door. Actually it sounded more like someone was trying to beat the damn thing down. He jumped off the bed like a scalded cat, making a grab for his pants on the way.

The pounding grew more intense. It had to be Nickie. He grunted as he pulled on his pants. His first thought was that she had somehow been hurt, but that didn't make much sense, not when she was capable of pounding hard enough to wake the dead. Other possible reasons for her appearance at this late hour raced through his mind and a sinking sensation surged through his gut. He tried to ignore them both, but the part of his brain that often annoyed him by coming up with ideas he didn't want to acknowledge insisted that the cause of such urgency could only be another ghostly misadventure.

By this time she had discovered the doorbell, and the melodious sound of its chimes now echoed off the walls and filled his ears. He grabbed for the shirt he'd had on earlier, pushing his arms into the sleeves.

"Just a minute!" he yelled. He felt along the wall to turn on the hall lights before starting down the stairs. He didn't want to break his neck, although the frantic knocking and ringing was starting to get to him. He quickly crossed the small foyer and threw open the heavy wooden door.

Before he could say a word, Nickie whipped open the screen door and flew past him into the room as though fifty demons were on her tail. "Nickie? What's wrong?"

"I don't believe it! I just don't believe it!" she muttered excitedly as she began pacing the small area between the couch and the window like a caged animal. "How did he do it? How did he get in? Oh, God, where is he now?"

"Is someone following you?" Griff demanded in a low urgent voice. When she didn't immediately answer he switched on the porch light and peered out into the night, his body tense and alert. But everything looked normal. He could even hear the crickets starting up again.

"Things like this don't happen to people, not in real life. Maybe I'm losing my mind." Nickie hid her face in her hands for a moment before lifting her head, her eyes suddenly blazing with conviction. "No, he was there all right. But where on earth did he come from?"

Griff crossed the room and grabbed her by the shoulders. With a small shake he forced her to look into his eyes. "Nickie, what's going on here?"

"Oh, Griff," she suddenly sobbed, throwing herself into his arms. "I saw him! He really exists!"

Her entire body shuddering, she clutched him around the waist as though he were the last life raft aboard the *Titanic*. When he heard her teeth begin to chatter, he couldn't stop himself from putting his arms around her and gathering her close.

They stood there like that for a long time, with Nickie's face buried against his chest. He could smell the fresh fragrance of her hair. Her body felt slender and very feminine in his embrace. He tried not to notice the press of her breasts against his chest, but it was impossible, and he discarded the idea without regret. After all, he'd just gotten settled into bed and he had to admit that a few tiny fantasies of sharing it with this woman had invaded a corner of his consciousness, although he'd made an attempt to dismiss them. But what guy wouldn't wonder about such things after meeting an attractive woman like Dominique DuPrés?

However, the reality of having her in his arms and clinging to him like ivy wasn't as easy to dismiss, especially when she seemed so content to stay there. He began to hope that perhaps this had nothing to do with anything supernatural. Maybe she thought she'd heard a prowler. Or maybe she had cooked up this crisis because she wanted to seduce him, and this was her way of doing it. He grinned in rueful amusement at his wishful thinking, but that didn't make it go away.

"All right, tell me what happened," he said softly, and although he tried, he couldn't keep the desire he felt stirring his nerve endings from turning his voice husky.

"Oh, Griff, I saw him! I saw the ghost!" Her eyes were wide with fright as she lifted them to stare into his. "He was dressed in an old-fashioned jacket and a ruffled shirt, and he held out his hand to me."

Griff couldn't help rolling his eyes as he called himself every kind of fool. He should have known better than to trust a DuPrés female, not when they had the annoying habit of seeing ghosts. Before he could think too much about it, he pushed her a safer distance away. His body vigorously protested the separation, but he ignored that, too.

"Come on, Nickie, cut it out," he said. He hadn't completely released her arms, and he gave her a little shake to emphasize his point. "I'm not my grandfather and I don't believe in ghosts. And, anyway, what do you expect me to do about it?"

His brain commanded his hands to let go of the soft flesh of her upper arms, but his fingers refused to cooperate. He found himself caressing her smooth skin, first with his fingertips and then with the curious wayward palms of his hands, moving them up and down her arms.

"What do you expect me to do about it?" he repeated, this time in a voice filled with meaning.

"N-nothing, I guess," she replied in resignation. Her brown eyes widened as she met his gaze and read the unmistakable message there. "Not that."

"Why not that?" he demanded in a coaxing voice. He tugged her up against him and she gasped when their bodies met. His flesh felt on fire and he wondered if she was having the same experience.

She began laughing and the sound had an underlying touch of hysteria. "I have to admit that terror and passion do have some things in common— pounding heart, sweaty palms, heavy breathing."

He had the grace to look chagrined. Talk about inappropriate timing. "Here, sit down," he said, leading her to the nearest chair and pushing her down into it before stalking over to the glass cabinet where a bottle of his grandfather's Irish whiskey still held a place of honor. Grabbing a nearby glass, he wiped it on the tail of his shirt, then sloshed a healthy serving into its streaky interior. She took it gratefully when he handed it to her.

She took a few small sips, coughing a little, but it seemed to calm her. She finished the contents of the glass as though taking a large shot of medicine.

"Whoa, go easy," he cautioned. "That's pretty lethal stuff."

She set the glass down before she leaned toward him in earnest supplication. "I know you don't believe me, but please, Griff, please try. I'm not making this up. I did see a ghost." He knew his expression was one of disbelief and saw her register the fact. She clenched her fists and softly pounded them against the tabletop. "What can I do to prove it to you?"

"Did you bring him with you?"

She made a face at him. "Ha ha, very funny."

In spite of his teasingly skeptical reply, he knew he was melting before the onslaught of her pleading pretty face and convincing body language. The terror in her eyes was certainly genuine. Something must have caused it, although he simply couldn't believe that it had been a ghost.

Perhaps there were some other physical phenomena that no one had thought to connect with Bellefleur. Just because Marie-Claire had insisted that the house was haunted didn't make it so. She hadn't been an easy woman to cross, as he had good cause to know. In any case, he was more determined than ever to get to the bottom of this while he was here.

"Are you all right now?" he asked.

She waved off his concern with a sweeping gesture. "What did your grandfather tell you about the ghost?"

"We never discussed it much. He knew how I felt about it."

"He must have told you something," she insisted.

"Yeah, I know a little bit about it."

"Well, come on, then. Give me a hand here."

Griff was adamant. "I'd rather not put any more ideas into your head."

"What? You think I saw this guy tonight just because you mentioned a ghost when we were out in the garden? Let me tell you, he was as real as you and me." She paused, frowning. "Well, maybe not quite that real, because I could see through him."

"Some people are very open to suggestion, and they don't even realize they are," Griff said in what he hoped was a neutral tone of voice. "I read a lot about these kinds of phenomena when my grandfather first told me. The mind is capable of playing tricks on us. It's not uncommon to see things, Nickie, especially at night. It's called a hypnagogic hallucination. It doesn't mean you're crazy or anything."

"Oh, swell. Thanks a lot. And I suppose next you're going to tell me that it runs in my family."

He held up his hands against that particular charge. "Hey, you said it, not me."

"If you're so sure there's no ghost, why don't you put your money where your mouth is and prove it? I can see that you're dying to become Bellefleur's own personal ghost buster.''

"And just how do I go about doing that?"

Nickie glared at him. "I don't know. You're the one who's so knowledgeable about hypna-whatevers.''

"All right," he said, standing up. "Let's go back to the house and try to figure this thing out." He reached out a hand to her. "Maybe you saw a reflection of a painting in a mirror. If I recall correctly, the walls of Bellefleur are covered with enough paintings to qualify as an art gallery.''

Nickie ignored his outstretched hand as she fiddled with her empty glass. "I didn't see him in one of the mirrored hallways.''

"Well, maybe it was some other kind of optical illusion." He wiggled his fingers invitingly. "Let's go check it out.''

"Please don't get the wrong idea, but would you mind if we just stayed here for a while?" Her voice wobbled slightly as she spoke and she avoided meeting his gaze. "I know it seems cowardly, but I don't think I can go back into that house just yet. Maybe I could sleep on your couch?''

He shrugged. "Sure.''

He dropped his hand to his side, slapping his palm against his thigh in frustration as he did so. Nickie's body gave a small jerk in response to the noise, but otherwise she remained motionless. She looked so abjectly miserable huddled against one corner of the sofa that Griff had the absurd desire to comfort her. It wasn't easy trying to keep a level head in this situation. He didn't want to encourage this ghost business, but he could also see that Nickie was badly shaken by whatever it was she thought she had seen.

"Tomorrow we'll go take a look, okay?" he offered gently. "In the meantime, you can use one of my T-shirts to sleep in if you want."

One corner of her mouth crooked up into a half smile. "Thank you, Griff. I really appreciate it."

"No problem."

He went upstairs to retrieve the shirt before he got into any more trouble. While he was there he grabbed a blanket and pillow from the linen closet. When he came back she was still in the same position.

"Here." He thrust the shirt into her hands. "It's wrinkled but it's clean."

"Thank you."

She clutched the material in her fingers, watching him as he set the blanket and pillow on the arm of the couch. She still appeared distracted and uneasy as she stared at him, and he wondered what she was thinking.

"Well," he said with a polite nod and a forced smile, "it's getting late. Good night, Nickie."

He was turning to leave when she reached out and grabbed his arm. The abruptness of her action combined with the burning touch of her fingers caused his skin to quiver in reaction. As he stared down into her wide brown eyes he realized that he wanted very badly to kiss her.

"Sorry," she said with a rueful laugh. "I...I guess I just needed a little more human contact."

His entire body tightened at her soft inflammatory words. "Come here, then, and let's do it right," he murmured in a husky voice as he pulled her off the couch and into his arms. Her nose only came up to his chin, but she raised her head so she could gaze into his face. He could feel her body trembling, tiny tremors that gained in intensity at the bottom of each shallow breath she drew; he didn't know if she was still frightened or if they affected each other more than might be good for either of them.

Suddenly her fingers convulsed against the small of his back. "Oh, Griff, I was petrified when I saw him. I thought my heart was going to pound itself right out of my body." She clutched at his belt, pressing her cheek against his chest as though she wanted to crawl inside him. Griff tried to soothe her by stroking her hair away from the side of her face.

"They always show stuff like this in the movies as though it was the easiest thing in the world," she said, her voice muffled against his shirt. "The heroine creeps around the haunted house with a candle and it always gets snuffed out right at the critical moment. Of course she bravely keeps going until she finally confronts the source of her terror and solves the mystery.

"Well, it wasn't easy at all," she continued, shaking her head emphatically. "It's not that he looked like a mean ghost. Actually he seemed quite nice and very handsome. I think he was trying to point to something. But let me tell you, it's just too nerve-racking to stand there staring at someone and yet right through him while he's trying to communicate with you! What am I going to do?" she wailed softly, gripping him harder. "How can I live in Bellefleur now, knowing he could pop up anytime?"

Griff made no reply to that, having none to give. He figured it was a rhetorical question, anyway.

"No way, no way," she murmured as though she was chanting. "He's not running me out of *my* house."

"Hush, Nickie, it's all right," Griff murmured soothingly as he patted her back. He was feeling pretty raw himself, and the pats soon graduated into soft rubbing motions that finally became full-fledged caresses. Damn, but he suddenly wanted to believe in her ghost! When he held her in his arms like this he found himself inclined to believe in anything. "We'll figure out something in the morning."

"You probably think I'm trying to seduce you into believing in this ghost," she declared. Her voice was tinged with the faintest trace of humor, which her hands clinging to his waist belied. "But I'm not, honest. I'll let go in a minute, I promise. And, anyway, I know you wouldn't fall for a trick like that."

"What makes you so sure?"

She looked up into his face with a wistful little smile. "Because you know you're going to be leaving, and you don't seem the type to start something you don't intend to finish."

"That shows what you know about it," he muttered, tightening his arms around her.

He groaned as he closed his eyes against the pure bliss of having such easy access to her body. She felt like heaven in his arms, so slender and yet so womanly. Once again he felt the softness of her breasts pressing into his ribs. He could also sense the questions pushing against his consciousness from somewhere in the back of his mind, but he ignored them.

He knew he didn't want to hear any more words. When he couldn't bear it another second, he lifted her chin with urgent fingers, bending down to press his mouth to hers.

And that was when everything exploded.

Maybe it was the late hour or the adrenaline rush from talking about ghosts. Or maybe it was the fact that Nickie had initiated their physical intimacy by making the first move, something that tended to send any normal red-blooded male into cosmic overdrive. Whatever it was, the moment his lips touched hers an instant connection was forged, one so strong and so electric he could actually feel the aftereffects of his response rippling outward along the surface of his skin.

She tasted of whiskey. He wasn't sure he could survive the heat and the pleasure they were generating as their mouths surged together again and again. But he was so far gone he didn't care, especially when she slid her arms along his chest and around his neck, bringing the rest of her body into melting contact with his.

He had always considered himself a gentleman, which meant he should give her the opportunity to withdraw if she wanted. He couldn't in good conscience take advantage of her while her emotional defenses were so weakened. No, he assured himself, over the clamor of his raging hormones, he would never do such a thing.

"We should stop," he muttered hoarsely against her lips. He tried to set a good example by following his own advice. He even got so far as to pull his mouth away from hers, although he took up the slack by kissing her face and the side of her neck. It was a valiant effort.

"Yes, you're right," she said on a sigh, turning her head to assist him as he headed toward her ear. She drew a deep shuddering breath. "At least you took my mind off the ghost."

The mention of the ghost brought Griff the rest of the way to his senses. What was he thinking of, getting involved like this with Nickie? She was the new owner of Bellefleur and a very rich woman, while he was the gardener's grandson. Maybe she didn't feel awkward about such things, but he did.

Besides, he had no intention of tangling with Bellefleur again. He'd already tried competing against the gardens for his grandfather's attention. He had come to terms with his feelings, but playing a role like that once was enough. Adding the persistent legend of the damned ghost to the mix was simply the clincher.

He moved away from her, trying not to appear too abrupt by allowing his hands to slide down her arms where he gave her fingers a squeeze before releasing them. His entire body ached, but he swallowed hard and gritted his teeth against it. "Look, we'd better get some sleep," he said. "Things always look different in the morning."

"Is that a promise?" she asked ruefully. She met his gaze, hiding nothing from him, allowing him to see she was still affected by the passion of their explosive kiss. Her brown eyes were soft and limpid, and her body language reinforced the message. He had to clench his hands against his sides to keep from pulling her back into his arms. She looked so vulnerable and so desirable....

In spite of his body's insistent urges, he managed a grin. "I hope I'm too smart to make a promise like that," he said. "There are far too many variables involved to even begin to predict the outcome."

"I love it when you talk probability to me."

He chuckled. "Sorry to be so pedantic. It must be the engineer in me. Well, good night, Nickie," he said, and headed for the stairs.

# Chapter Four

When Nickie awoke the next morning, she sensed she was alone in the cottage. She listened carefully for a few moments just to be certain, but she couldn't hear a sound. Already she could feel the questions whirling around in her head, eagerly crowding forward for a share of her attention. She ruthlessly squashed them down, concentrating instead on stretching her body from head to toe to ease the stiffness of a night spent on the sofa.

It was a losing battle. Just because she wasn't ready to analyze the events of last night and her behavior afterward didn't mean a thing. She intended to forget about the ghost and carry on as though nothing had happened. In the light of day that seemed the easiest solution. This was where she belonged, and no ghost was going to run her out of Bellefleur no matter how hard he tried!

In spite of everything, or more likely because of it, she discovered she was starving. Sliding off the sofa, she grabbed her clothes, holding them against her as she crept down the hall toward the small bathroom located beneath the stairs. Once she was safely inside with the door half-closed she called Griff's name just in case her instincts had been wrong. He didn't answer.

Ten minutes later, dressed and ready to face the world, she marched into the kitchen. The smell of freshly brewed coffee was the first thing to greet her, and she gratefully poured herself a cup from the pot on the counter. As she stood there sipping the hot brew, she glanced at the clock on the wall. It was already after eight.

She wondered what time Griff had gotten up. An empty grocery sack lay across the table. She found that the refrigerator contained bacon, eggs and a fresh loaf of bread for toast. She wasn't sure if the items were a hint for her to make him breakfast, or if he intended to return to fix his own, but she wasn't insulted. She figured it was the least she could do under the circumstances.

She quickly went to work. Even as thoughts of Griff's kisses filled her mind, the events that had precipitated her journey across the front lawn of Bellefleur to the cottage also began pushing into her consciousness, as she had known they would. Her short reprieve was over.

So she'd been scared. So what, she thought with a frown as she broke eggs into an old chipped ceramic bowl. She'd been vulnerable and had allowed Griff to kiss her. It wasn't the end of the world. Griff had succumbed to the sparks that had been so evident between them, and then he had backed off, just as she'd suspected he would. She had no fears that he would march back into the kitchen and try to take up where he'd left off.

She rolled her eyes, but her grin was filled with soft regret. Sure she had fallen fast and hard for Griff. Maybe it couldn't be undone, but at least she could keep it from going any further. Her own peace of mind was at stake here. Having a darn ghost in her house was bad enough; she didn't need any more trouble.

When the bacon was almost done, she turned down the burner and went in search of Griff.

She found him weeding a flower bed whose various colored plants formed a geometric design. He'd only done half, and already the improvement was evident and beautiful. His shirt was draped over the small statue of a wood nymph, which graced the center of the circular bed. He had his back to her and didn't hear her approach, giving her time to watch him. Her eyes took in the lean muscles of his shoulders as they rippled under his smooth skin. His black hair looked soft and tousled. She longed to touch him.

Instead, she spoke to break the sensual spell. "Good morning."

He quickly glanced over his shoulder. "Good morning, Nickie."

"I hope you haven't already eaten."

"No."

"Good. Listen, I made use of the eggs and bacon you had in your refrigerator and made us some breakfast."

He rose slowly to his feet, his eyes glinting like green fire in the early-morning sunlight. She tried not to stare at his broad heavily muscled chest, but she couldn't help stealing a quick once-over. She noticed that his gaze also roamed up and down her body before resettling on her face. "You didn't have to do that."

She shrugged. "I was hungry and I figured you must be, too."

"Yeah. We had quite an exciting time last night, didn't we?"

She felt embarrassed warmth flood her face, mostly because she wasn't sure just which parts of the evening he was including in his definition of "exciting." She said, "You'd better come on. It'll be ready in a couple of minutes."

He followed her back to the cottage. While he washed up at the sink, she poured the beaten eggs into the pan and pushed down the bread in the toaster. A few minutes more and she was setting the plates on the table. Griff had refilled their coffee cups and she had added the finishing touches to breakfast, so there was nothing left for her to do except seat herself opposite him. His thick dark hair looked as though he had only run his fingers through it, in lieu of a comb, and his sexy morning face badly needed a shave. Neither circumstance took anything away from his heady masculine appeal.

What should have been comfortable and domestic was unnerving and strange, mostly because she didn't know what Griff was thinking. His countenance gave nothing away, while his tough-guy handsomeness provided an inscrutable mask for him to hide behind. She only hoped her expression cloaked her emotions as thoroughly.

They didn't say much during the meal. She asked about the garden and he complimented the meal. As soon as they were finished, he pushed back his plate.

"I see you've recovered from your ghost," he said, watching her quietly.

She'd known it was coming and she supposed it was kind of him to allow her to finish her breakfast in peace before beginning the attack. "He's not *my* ghost, but yes, I'm doing all right this morning," she said with a shrug and an awkward little smile. "The light of day is a great cure for apparitions. The problem is that it might only be temporary."

"You know I've never heard of a ghost quite like the one you say you saw."

"What do you mean?" she answered warily.

"From all the things I've ever read or heard, ghosts usually start out slowly—you know, a few noises in the hallway, some thumps on the stairs. Then, after they've built up a nice reserve of credibility, they really buckle down to business and begin their haunting in earnest. That's when they appear in their full glory."

"I didn't know you were such an expert on the subject," she commented tartly.

"Like I told you last night, I've checked into a few things over the years."

Nickie leaned her arms on the table and sighed. Everything connected with the incident sounded silly in the light of day, and she wished they could just forget about ghosts for a while. She glanced at Griff, but he didn't seem eager to drop the subject.

"Maybe he's more impatient than the average ghost," she said.

"Impatient for what?"

"For someone to haunt, of course," she retorted with a cheeky grin. Her only defense against Griff's skepticism and her own ambivalent feelings was to joke about it. "He's probably been waiting since my aunt died for a nice gullible victim like me to scare the starch out of." Suddenly she shivered, remembering how the specter's pale lips had moved. She quickly shook away the image.

She suddenly couldn't sit still any longer, so she jumped to her feet and began clearing the dishes from the table. Griff's usually sharp-eyed gaze was somewhat subdued as he followed her movements around the kitchen. It was clear that his thoughts were engaged elsewhere. He was slouched casually in his chair, yet he still exuded vitality and more than a dose of good old-fashioned virility.

Her flippant attitude about the whole episode was only a front, but it seemed to be working at the moment. In any case it kept her from doing what she really wanted to do, which was throw herself on Griff's mercy the way she had last night and beg him to make it all go away. The way he had tossed off his cool questions this morning assured her it would be a futile effort.

"So, what do we do now?" she asked. She finished running hot water over the dishes she'd piled in the sink, then tossed the dishrag over the faucet and turned to face him.

"We go over to the house and check things out."

She swallowed hard, not particularly eager to return to the scene, but knowing she must no matter what the cost to her equilibrium. The sooner she pushed herself through the initial discomfort of having to replay last night's events in all their glorious detail, the sooner she could go on with her life in her new home as she intended to live it. Maybe Griff would be able to show her it was all a misunderstanding.

"I hope you realize that this business only started after you arrived," she said, hoping to put him on the defensive for a change. "I was doing just fine until then."

He didn't take the bait. "Hey, that's a possibility we haven't considered. Maybe someone is pulling a ghostly prank on you." He frowned thoughtfully. "But who? And more to the point, why?"

Nickie hadn't thought of such a mundane possibility as a human suspect, mostly because she'd been too wrapped up in trying to come to terms with what she'd seen. But she gave his statement careful consideration now.

"Maybe that lawyer has a plan to get me to sell, so he came up with a plan to scare me off," she said. She felt foolish uttering such a wild unsubstantiated charge, but it was the first idea that popped into her head. Then she shuddered as an image of the apparition slipped past the barrier she'd erected in her mind to keep him at bay, his hand held out to her in that beseeching manner that still gave her heart palpitations. "If that's his game, I must say it's working."

"You've been watching too much TV. I know Dutch, and he would never pull such a stunt. You'll have to come up with something better than that."

"If you ask me, the damn ghost has the best motive of all. He likes having the house to himself, and he wants to keep it that way. Which is fine with me," she added, clenching her jaw in determination, "because whatever he does, he's not going to make me change my plans."

"That's the spirit," Griff murmured in amusement.

She wished she could think of something clever to say, some remark that would wipe that smirk off his face, but her mind was blank. Instead, she glared over her shoulder at the dishes in the sink wondering why women always had such a compulsion to clean up after everyone. She quickly decided that Griff could do his own darn housework.

"Have you got any suggestions for where we go from here?" she asked as she moved away from the counter.

"Sure."

He sounded very confident and much too cheerful, Nickie decided. "What?" she asked suspiciously.

"For starters, we quit arguing about hypothetical things and get started looking for a more plausible explanation for your ghost." Griff snapped his fingers as though to indicate it was the easiest thing in the world. "The sooner we get to the bottom of this, the better."

"He is not *my* ghost," she retorted, laughing.

"He is until further notice." His eyes met hers and they sparkled like cut green glass. "No one else wants to claim him."

Nickie rolled her eyes, but refrained from commenting as she followed Griff from the kitchen toward the front door. He held the screen door open for her. As they stepped outside into the bright morning sunlight, she found it hard to believe that she was going on a quest to disprove an occurrence she had witnessed with her own two eyes and experienced with every particle of her being.

She glanced at Griff. He looked serious and thoughtful as he paced alongside her, but then he usually did. She didn't mind his serious expression, because she liked to see the startling contrast when he smiled. She had also enjoyed the sparks of green fire she had noticed in the depths of his eyes as he'd gazed down at her last night. She found that she wanted to bring that expression back again. So much for her plan to remain aloof, but at least her speculations kept her from dwelling on the ghost every waking minute.

When they reached the top of the porch stairs, Griff gestured for her to precede him. She didn't want to, but she forced herself to open the door, trying to squelch the sensations that assaulted her as she remembered her last time here.

"All right. Where did you see him, Nickie?"

"It was upstairs on the second floor."

"Come on then."

As if he knew how agitated she was, he reached for her hand, enveloping it in the warmth of his. "Don't worry," he said with a smile. "I don't think ghosts make house calls during daylight hours."

She smiled wanly. She didn't have the heart to point out that the dust cloud had appeared in the heat of the afternoon. There was still the possibility that the swirl of particles had nothing to do with the handsome figure she had later seen. She held on tightly as Griff led her up the stairs.

The fifth stair creaked as usual. Before she was ready, they had reached the landing.

"Nice piece of furniture," Griff said, nodding his head in the direction of the graceful Louis XIV table. "I don't know a lot about antiques, but I can appreciate quality when I see it."

Nickie gasped in horror as she stared at the vase of cut flowers that sat in the center of the tabletop.

"Don't tell me it's not genuine," he said, his eyebrows lifting in good-natured humor.

"Oh, it's a genuine Louis Quatorze all right," she managed to croak above the pounding of her heart.

"Then what is it?"

She pointed mutely at the flowers.

"Yes, they're very pretty," he acknowledged.

"I didn't put them there."

"What do you mean?"

"I mean I didn't put them there," she repeated impatiently. "I have no idea where they came from."

He pulled her along with him as he moved forward to inspect the colorful bouquet. "They look like they came from the garden," he said, fingering the petals of a glossy pink geranium. "You probably cut them yesterday and forgot all about it after what happened last night."

She shook her head vigorously. "I didn't take any flowers from the garden. I wouldn't even know where to begin."

"Then maybe Dutch hired someone to clean up the house before you arrived."

"No. I cleaned the house myself. There was dust all over everything."

"All right," he murmured soothingly. She wondered if he could tell she was nursing a mild case of hysterics. "Who else beside you and Dutch has the key to this place?"

"No one else."

"Well, someone put them there," he stated emphatically. He was a natural problem-solver, and she could see that it irked him not to have an immediate solution to this one. "Were they there last night?"

"I don't know." She pressed her lips together, her brow furrowed with anxiety. "I don't think so, but I can't say for sure. I know they weren't there yesterday afternoon."

He leaned forward so he could better read her expression. "Don't even say it."

"Say what?"

"You think the ghost put them here, don't you?"

She ducked her head, avoiding his gaze. "I..."

He let go of her hand, instead grabbing her arms and turning her to face him. The laser effect of his direct green-eyed gaze was in full force. "I don't believe this! I suppose he was so smitten with you that he ran right out to the garden and picked you some flowers."

"I never even thought about that possibility," she replied honestly. Her eyes widened as the soft floral scent of the bouquet wafted past her nose, the smell she had always associated with Bellefleur. If the ghost had managed such a feat, he had more likely done it for Bellefleur than for her, but she wasn't about to mention that passing theory to Griff.

"Never mind." He dropped his hands from her arms, running one distractedly through his thick black hair. "I'll talk to Dutch about it, okay? In the meantime, let's just stick to the cold hard facts. Now, where were you standing when you saw it?''

She led him the rest of the way up the stairs to the second floor, indicated her previous evening's location, then leaned back against the wall to watch him investigate. A sudden wave of calm washed over her as she realized with a start that she wasn't afraid anymore, for two very heartfelt reasons.

No matter how much she wanted it or how hard she tried, the indelible image of the ghost of Bellefleur refused to erase itself from her memory. How could she forget the experience when every eloquent move her gentleman caller had made kept replaying in her head like a scene from a movie? Although she might doubt the wisdom of some of her responses, she never once questioned the essence of what she had seen. It might turn out to be an illusion, perhaps some kind of inner vision, but accepting the reality of her experience, deciding to trust her own senses and intuition, imparted a feeling of serenity and power that was unlike anything she'd ever known.

Oddly enough, the second reason was Griff's healthy skepticism. She found that it provided a solid backdrop against which she could chart her experience. She wasn't sure if she could ever prove the reality of the ghost to him, but simply being forced to try kept her grounded in reality. In fact, the more he scoffed, the better she liked it. Any ghost who could stand up to the rigorous investigation Griff would give him deserved to be believed in.

In any case, the quest had already progressed too far for her to turn her back on it. "What do you think?" she asked with a smile.

He was down at the other end of the hall, checking out every possible angle of approach. "I can't see anything immediately obvious, but then I didn't figure it would be simple. What about this guy?" He pointed to a large painting in an ornate frame that hung over a small gilded table in the hallway.

"What about him?" From where she was standing, she could only see the side of the frame. She strolled over to stand next to Griff in front of the painting, knowing what she would see when she got there. "That's Louis XIV, the Sun King. He built Versailles."

They stood a moment, staring at the delicate features of the man in the portrait. He was shown seated on a small thronelike stool holding a scepter in his right hand, his left leg slightly extended. He was wearing a royal purple cape with an ermine collar. The body of the cloak was embroidered with a host of fleur-de-lis in gold thread. He also had on an elaborate white powdered wig.

"That's not what my late-night visitor looked like, if that's what you mean. The ghost was tall and much more handsome, and he wasn't wearing a wig. Besides, from where I was standing, there's no way I could have seen that painting."

He shrugged. "I didn't think you'd go for it, but I figured I'd ask."

"What now, Sherlock?"

"We wait for it to happen again."

"Suppose it doesn't?"

"Then your troubles are over. In the meantime, I'm going to get back to work."

ALTHOUGH SHE DIDN'T GET a lot accomplished, Nickie forced herself to spend the entire day in the upstairs study. It was hard to concentrate on her illustration of a green iguana when she spent most of her time looking over her shoulder. The house was filled with creaks and twitches, and she found herself jumping at every tiny noise. Much to her relief, the ghost made no appearance.

She had invited Griff over for dinner after his first day of hard labor in the fields. She figured she owed it to him. At half-past six, she gave up trying to look busy and headed gratefully downstairs to heat up the soup Velma had brought over and fix some sandwiches. She knew Griff wanted to take advantage of every hour of daylight, so she didn't expect him before seven.

Modern appliances had been added to the kitchen sometime during the sixties, but the room still retained its early nineteenth-century spaciousness and elegance, as did the rest of the house. When she was done in the kitchen, she wandered into the hallway that led to the formal dining room. Maybe the ghost could only hang around the upper floors, like an upstairs maid, she thought as her gaze took in the huge dining room table surrounded by twelve hand-carved wooden chairs.

She glanced into the front parlor, with its French doors opening onto the veranda. It contained a piano and a hand-painted card table. She had already peeked into the drawers and discovered a deck of cards. This hadn't been considered a particularly large house by the standards of the time, but of course families were much bigger then.

A knock brought her out of her reverie and she hurried to answer the front door. Griff stood there, dressed in black jeans and a white shirt, his hair still damp from a shower. He looked good enough to be included on the menu. He clutched a large bouquet of pink and white flowers in one hand.

"I had to trim some of the flower beds back," he explained as he handed them to her. "It seemed a shame to waste them."

"They're lovely. Thank you." She gestured him inside. "Come on back to the kitchen. I figured we'd eat there. Unless you prefer to sit at a table for twelve."

"The kitchen's fine. I'm sure it's fancier than what I usually make do with."

"Ah, the life of a vagabond. According to Velma, you thrive on it."

He smiled. "Living out of a suitcase and surviving on take-out food isn't all it's cracked up to be." He sat down at the table, a lovely and solid oak set with sturdy matching chairs obviously meant for the servants. Nickie had already decided it was just as beautiful in its hand-hewn simplicity as some of the fancier pieces. But then everything at Bellefleur was beautiful.

She set a steaming bowl of soup in front of him and indicated the plate of sandwiches. "Velma contributed the soup and I made the sandwiches."

"Looks great," he said, and obviously meant it as he proceeded to consume sandwiches and soup in rapid workmanlike fashion.

Nickie proceeded more slowly. "How's the garden coming along?"

"Pretty good. I've started on the parts closest to the house—those that you see immediately."

"Good idea."

"The fountain has a clog somewhere in the main water pipe, but I'm working on it. How did your afternoon go?" he asked as he bit into his third sandwich. He seemed to have assuaged the worst of his hunger; his brisk pace had mellowed.

"Fine." She paused, then added truthfully, "Well, not that fine. I had a pretty hard time concentrating. I know ghosts aren't supposed to appear during the day, but I still kept thinking he was going to pop up at any minute."

"Why don't you work in the cottage?"

"Why should I? This is my house now. Besides, that would defeat the purpose—we're trying to see the ghost again, not avoid him."

"True. But you can't let it disrupt your work schedule."

She shrugged noncommittally.

Silence reigned while he polished off the sandwich. After wiping his mouth, he tossed the paper napkin she had given him onto his empty plate. "Why don't you use the cottage during the day so you can work in peace. You can return here at night. That's when things are more likely to occur, anyway."

"No way," she replied in a firm voice, trying to sound casual and unconcerned.

Griff wasn't fooled. "What is it? What's the matter?" he demanded.

She smoothed her fingers over the wooden tabletop, studiously avoiding his gaze. She hadn't meant to ask, but somehow the words came tumbling out of her mouth. "I would feel much better if you stayed here with me. You could sleep in the only other bed besides mine that has sheets that actually fit."

She raised her gaze to meet his, expecting to see impatience or even disgust at her cowardice stamped all over his darkly handsome features, but his expression showed only interested speculation. "That's an idea."

"Then I wouldn't have to run all the way across the front lawn to tell you next time something happens," she pointed out with a small self-deprecating smile. Of course, that was the least of her worries, but it sounded logical and she knew logic was the best way to appeal to a man like Griff.

He grinned in return, his eyes glinting with good humor and some other, more elemental emotion she couldn't quite label. "All right."

"Great." She nodded in brisk approval, trying not to let her relief show—and ignoring her quickened pulses at the thought of Griff's spending an entire night only a couple of doors away from her. "You know, if you stay here you might get to see the ghost, too."

"I'd much rather you see the ghost and I do the comforting."

"Yes, well, if it happens again I don't think I'll fall apart as completely as I did the first time."

"Too bad."

Nickie began picking up the empty bowls, ignoring the implications of what he was saying. She knew he was teasing her the way most guys would under similar circumstances. He didn't really mean it, although that sobering conclusion didn't erase her longing to be held in his arms again. She was too honest with herself to insist that all she was seeking there was a safe haven.

"Don't worry, I can handle these few dishes," she told him when he began helping her.

"All right, thanks. I'll go get my things."

After he left, Nickie made quick work of cleaning the kitchen. Then she loitered downstairs, more grateful than she cared to admit that Griff had so readily agreed to play bodyguard. As long as she wasn't entirely alone, she knew she could handle the ghost. After all, didn't familiarity breed contempt? She couldn't imagine herself ever mustering a calm sense of superiority in the presence of the handsome poised apparition, but she hoped she could at least act like the rational, capable adult she considered herself to be.

She wasn't sure whether she wanted the ghost to return or not. She realized that her fear of encountering it again was disappearing bit by bit every time she ran the possibility through her mind. After all, no real harm had come to her, except for getting kissed by Griff. Now she knew just how attached to him she could become, given the slightest encouragement.

Some people might claim she was playing with fire, but she saw no reason to stop herself at this safe early stage. The man was involved in her ghost hunt just as she'd hoped. If it forced her to get to know him better than she might otherwise have done, well, she also knew all the tricks for keeping her distance. He was the only link she had to Bellefleur's past, and as such he was invaluable. Her strategy was to get him to open up and tell her everything he knew about his grandfather, her great-aunt and the ghost—no matter how foolish or impractical he thought it. If she stuck to ghost hunting with him, nothing more and nothing less, she should come out of this relatively unscathed.

By the time Griff returned to the house it was dark. She led him upstairs to his room, pausing just across the threshold to allow him time to absorb the full impact of its mauve-and-apple-green decor. A room like this could be overwhelming to someone who didn't actually live here, as she had good cause to know.

He walked to the bed, tossing the clothes he'd brought onto its broad surface. It wasn't as grand as the huge canopied affair in her room, but it was still a bed to be reckoned with. An ivory-and-mauve silk hanging shielded the side that faced the door while delicate gilt scrollwork along the headboard added a further touch of luxury.

She watched as his gaze took in the painting hanging in the alcove directly across the room from the foot of the bed. It was a rendering of a partially clothed personification of Night holding aloft a torch, while the Bird of Darkness crouched like a malevolent vulture at her feet. As an inducement to soothe the occupant to sleep, Nickie feared it was a decided failure.

He finally set his small overnight case on the floor next to the matching gilded table, a bemused expression on his face as he continued to absorb the details of the room. He looked lost, as if he'd wandered onto the set of a movie with no director to tell him where to stand or when to say his lines. She loved every detail of Bellefleur, but she could imagine how fussy and impractical the place must seem to a modern no-nonsense engineer like Griff.

His head tilted back as his gaze followed an inlaid marble Corinthian column. At the juncture where it appeared to be holding up the painted sky, two naked smiling cherubs peered down playfully from their celestial perch. "I'm not sure if your peace of mind is worth this sacrifice," he noted dryly.

"Once the lights go out you won't even notice them," she assured him.

She crossed to the chiffonier and opened several drawers before she finally found the one containing the extra blankets. She could see Griff behind her, reflected in the mirror attached to the top of the tall wooden structure. As if he knew she was watching him, his eyes met hers in the glass. For some reason, this struck her as very intimate, and she quickly glanced away. With brisk motions she closed the drawer and turned to face him.

"All the comforts of home," he said, a teasing glint in his eyes as he gestured around the baroque ornateness of the room. "Now I know what's meant by that old metaphor 'a bird in a gilded cage.'"

She chuckled because the notion of Griff in any kind of cage seemed ludicrous. "Can you think of anything else you might need?" She immediately realized her question could be interpreted on another, more elemental level, but she ignored its sexual implications and schooled her expression into one of bland inquiry, playing the role of polite hostess to the hilt.

His eyes gleamed in acknowledgment of her predicament. The painted green highlights of the room emphasized their color and depth. "I think I'm as set as I'm ever going to be...tonight."

"Great," she said as she headed for the door. If she hadn't been so attuned to every nuance of his speech and actions, she might not have noticed that slight hesitation before he'd added that last revealing word. As it was, she tried to ignore both the tenseness in her body and the thick sensuality she could feel emanating from Griff. She swore it filled the entire room, right up to the cherubs floating on their billowy white clouds.

"See you tomorrow," she added brightly as she made her escape into the hallway.

She'd known he was potent at close range, but it had suddenly become more than she could comfortably handle for long stretches of time. It had been much easier when they were arguing about the ghost. She would have to make sure that from now on they stuck to that topic whenever they were together. She didn't like the idea that things weren't going to be as smooth and uncomplicated as she'd originally intended. She hadn't reckoned on her response to Griff, which was turning out to be more than a surface attraction to a handsome male.

She walked quickly to her room, refusing to allow her mind to dwell on just how short the distance really was. And yet she admitted she was vastly relieved not to be alone in the house. These ghostly visitations were still too new for her to feel comfortable about them, no matter how often she tried to scold herself into acting as if they were the most normal occurrences in the world.

Half an hour later she sat on the edge of her huge four-poster bed, dangling her feet over the sides. Her toes barely reached the worn wooden stool she had to use every night to climb onto the mattress, and it made her feel like a child in a grown-up world. As if the breathtaking grandeur and beauty of Bellefleur wasn't enough to fuel any woman's dreams, the appearance of the ghost had served to further propel her into an unusual state of mind, one with that magical sense of openness and wonder children always possess in such abundance. She couldn't seem to stop herself at times from believing that anything was possible. Yet that was a dangerous notion when she considered her vulnerability to Griff's presence in her life, a presence that could only be temporary.

Her gaze wandered to the tall nightstand, where a small photograph held the place of honor in front of a Venetian lamp. The original papier-mâché frame, with its gaudy yellow and red flowers, that she had chosen as a child had long since been replaced by a simple acrylic holder. Nickie reached over and picked it up, fingering the smooth contours of the plastic as she stared at a younger version of herself standing on the front steps of Bellefleur.

She could still recall her shock and pleased surprise when the photograph had arrived in the mail several weeks after her visit to Bellefleur, along with a brief note from Marie-Claire. The note had long since disappeared, but she had carried the picture with her everywhere, never even allowing it to be packed up by the moving men with the rest of her belongings.

Over the years, as she'd been shunted from place to place, it had become a sort of a talisman, a reminder that she could lay claim to a permanent base in her life, that she belonged somewhere other than the next rented house or the next new school with its unfamiliar faces. By the time she left her teenage years behind, she'd become inured to the ever-present sense of impermanence that cloaked her life. But the photograph remained.

She replaced it on the nightstand with a small sigh and a crooked smile. She had expected Bellefleur to embrace her with open arms because she cared about the place. What she hadn't counted on was the ghostly greeting she had received so soon after arriving. She wondered if each new tenant had been welcomed in the same startling fashion.

On that note, she turned off the light and snuggled down between the soft cotton sheets.

*Chapter Five*

Nickie awoke the next morning with a sense of well-being. She had slept soundly and, as far as she could recall, dreamlessly. No ghost had shown up to disturb her sleep. It was almost as if he knew he had terrified her, and had decided to keep away.

She heard noises from the kitchen so she quickly got dressed. She wanted to catch Griff before he left. Heavens, but the man was an early riser. It was barely six-thirty. Still, she couldn't complain, not when the sun was already shining through her window, inviting her to come and behold another glorious summer day.

As she hurried along the hallway on her way to the stairs, she suddenly realized that a babble of bird sounds was beginning to take precedence over the early-morning stillness she had been savoring. If she didn't know better, she'd have said that the birds were holding a singing contest. Their various warbling melodies and shrill cries chased each other up and down the musical scale. Although each individual note was sweet, the overall clashing discord was unavoid-able. Too many members of the vast feathered population of Bellefleur were vying for the honor of who could trill the loudest.

She recalled leaving the window of her study open yesterday. Of course, that would explain why it seemed as though the birds were cavorting right inside the house. Just to be sure that wasn't the case, she paused to glance into the room. Her heart skipped a beat at the sight that greeted her.

It seemed the ghost was also an early riser.

This time he had his back to her as he stood staring out the window. He was dressed as before in a quietly elegant coat and breeches. The toe of one booted foot was propped casually against the floor as he leaned one hip against the wall in a relaxed manner. Beyond him she could see several birds hopping from branch to branch in what seemed like avian excitement.

By this time their cries had reached a crescendo. Was it possible that the birds could see him? Were they sensitive to ghosts the way dogs and cats supposedly were? If that was true, they weren't flying away from him in fear but, instead, were singing their little hearts out.

*Who are you?* she wondered, the question burning in her brain even above the thumping of her heart. Before she could make a move, he slowly dissolved right before her eyes, first turning into a million light-filled particles and then completely disappearing. She blinked but he was truly gone, and something inside her ached at the loss. Part of her mind quietly noted that the noise quotient of the birds had returned to its more usual level.

Not knowing what else to do, she continued along the hallway and headed down the stairs. She was still dazed when she entered the kitchen.

Griff was standing there, in a pose reminiscent of the ghost, his back turned to her as he gazed out the back window sipping his coffee. He heard her approach and turned to greet her immediately. She found she wanted to touch him, just to feel someone solid.

"Good morning," he said. He pointed with his half-filled mug at the counter. "There's more coffee."

"I'm going to need it," she stated glumly.

"Everybody needs a good jolt of caffeine in the morning."

"Yeah, well, I need it more than most." She drew a deep breath, and then because there was no delicate way to introduce the topic, she didn't bother to try. "I just saw him again," she announced.

Griff showed no outward reaction of shock as he remained across the room from her, casually cradling the mug in his hands. "Oh?"

"Yes, 'oh.' And you don't have to tread so carefully, as if I'm some kind of nut case. You can say what you think." She met his gaze unflinchingly.

His mouth crooked up at the corner and he looked genuinely amused. "Thank you. I appreciate that."

She tilted her head, a militant gleam appearing in her eyes. "That's good, because there's no way anyone is ever going to convince me I didn't just see a ghost."

Griff nodded. She couldn't tell from his expression what he was thinking, but his next question was neutral enough. "What happened?"

"Nothing really." She frowned. "He was standing looking out the window in the study. As soon as I spotted him, he just faded away into nothing." She knew her awestruck amazement at the ghost's disappearing act must be stamped all over her features.

"No gestures, no attempts to communicate?"

She shook her head. "He never even turned around."

"I see."

"I wish you had—seen him, that is." She began rummaging through the cabinets for a mug and proceeded to pour herself some coffee. "I've never been predisposed to believe in ghosts. I've always been a normal everyday person who went about her life in a normal everyday fashion. I didn't ask for this."

"I'm sure you didn't."

"But you still don't believe me."

He gestured helplessly. "Put yourself in my place, Nickie. It's not that I don't want to believe you. I'm simply trying to keep a cool head and look at all the facts dispassionately."

"I see. And I suppose one of the more salient facts is that your grandfather, who happens to believe in ghosts, never saw him?"

"Nickie—"

"And my aunt, whom you heartily disliked, supposedly did see him?"

"What the hell has that got to do with anything?" he exclaimed. "I don't dislike you!"

That brought her up short. It wasn't much of a declaration, but it still sent a sweet rush of warmth up her throat and into her cheeks. Her gaze flew to meet his, in spite of her resolve.

Without taking his eyes from her face, he walked across the kitchen, slapping his mug onto the counter before coming to stand in front of her. Grasping her hands, he began rubbing small circles in the centers of her palms with his thumbs, his movements firm and hypnotic. His skin felt warm and slightly rough. "I want to get to the bottom of this just as much as you do."

"I think your idea of what's at the bottom differs from mine."

He smiled, giving her hands a squeeze, but he didn't seem in a hurry to release them. "Maybe. But although we each perhaps have a different perception of what's going on, in the end neither one of us can change the facts. Once everything is brought to light, we'll have to agree."

"No matter what the outcome?"

"No matter what the outcome."

Hah, she thought, grinning. She knew he expected one of his two suppositions to eventually be proved correct. He thought that it was either some sort of optical illusion or that she was imagining things. In fact, he was so sure some physical principle was at work here he figured he could afford to be generous with her.

She clamped down her urge to laugh out loud. She couldn't wait to see his face when he found out that the ghost of Bellefleur was real. She only hoped it wouldn't shock him too much.

He had stopped his soothing motions and now gave her hands another squeeze before he released them. "Will you call me the next time something happens? If I'm downstairs I'll hear you, I promise."

"Sure." She was feeling cocky now. "I can't guarantee that he'll stick around until you get there. He might not want to scare you."

"What makes you say that?" he asked. Nickie could see that he had decided to humor her for the time being, but she imagined the situation must be testing his patience, something he didn't seem to have in abundance.

"I think he realized he scared me pretty badly the other day. This time I had the feeling he knew I was there but didn't want to frighten me again. That's why he disappeared without turning around."

"Jeez, Nickie," he muttered, his good humor vanishing as quickly as it had appeared. "Don't you think you're getting carried away here? Seeing a ghost is bad enough, but bestowing him with qualities of kindness and thoughtfulness is too much."

"Not really." She shrugged cheerfully. "It's only too obvious he's a gentleman ghost. And he does have a kind face," she added with a wistful little smile. "Not to mention handsome."

Griff looked even more disgruntled at that ingenuous remark. "I'd better head out to the gardens."

"Don't you want any breakfast?"

"No."

"I'll make you some lunch if you want."

"Okay. Thanks."

"No trouble."

She watched him march out of the kitchen, a thoughtful expression on her face. Things had gone from interesting to double intriguing, from one handsome male presence to two. She picked up her coffee, tasted it and, with a grimace, placed it into the microwave to heat. She hated tepid coffee.

Once again she ran through the brief sequence of events in the study. Had she really seen the ghost's shoulders stiffen slightly when she'd appeared in the doorway? Now that she thought about it, she was positive she had. And he had dissolved almost as soon as she'd set eyes on him. Why else would he have left except for her presence? It was already daylight, so it wasn't as though he were a vampire who had to avoid the sun.

But none of these speculations was as interesting as wondering about the ghost's identity. She was getting tired of referring to him as "the ghost." Maybe she should just ask him who he was, she thought with a crooked smile of amusement. Even as a small chuckle escaped her, a faint shiver ran down her spine at the thought of carrying on such an intimate, not to mention ghostly, conversation. He didn't seem able to speak, but maybe she hadn't really tested that possibility.

Whatever he hoped to accomplish with his presence, she knew with a deep gut instinct that he had no intention of harming her. And she also realized that nothing was going to stop her from investigating this ghost six ways to Sunday, beginning with a search for his identity.

It never hurt to know exactly whom you were dealing with.

GRIFF WAS STILL MUTTERING under his breath as he unlocked the door to the shed. As he gathered the gardening tools he needed for his work today, carrying them outside into the bright sunlight, he couldn't help glancing over his shoulder at the row of second-floor windows, although he wouldn't admit to himself that he was looking for a face. All was quiet, both there and everywhere else he scanned.

He decided he must be more shaken than he cared to admit. The more he thought about it, the more he realized that this entire setup seemed designed to drive him crazy. He was a firm realist, practical and hard-headed, as he'd been told often enough. All this blathering on about ghosts was beginning to get to him. If he wasn't careful, he would end up on one of those TV shows like "Mysteries of the Unknown," making a complete fool of himself.

He loaded equipment into the wheelbarrow, barely noticing the warmth of the sun on his back or the gentle caress of the sweet-scented early-morning air. The sounds of birds and insects, something he usually appreciated, had faded into mere background noise. His tumultuous thoughts took precedence over everything else.

He headed along the walkway toward the main pavilion, his footsteps crunching on the gravel. The front axle of the wheelbarrow squeaked, but he paid no heed to the intrusive noise, going over once again his impression of Nickie's character. Although he hadn't known her long, he'd immediately sensed a core of integrity in her. He believed she was telling the truth as she'd experienced it. Therein lay the crux of the matter.

All this talk about the ghost of Bellefleur, along with her childhood experiences with a stranger, had somehow made her susceptible to seeing something that resembled a human figure. With each further "visitation" she became more convinced, and therefore more susceptible to further sightings. That had to be the answer; any other alternative was alarming and impossible. Just because he wanted to kiss her and hold her was no excuse to start believing in the impossible. And yet...

And yet nothing, he assured himself, his eyes narrowing in determination. He raised the hoe over his head as he aimed a deadly and satisfying blow at a clod of dirt. There had to be another explanation and he intended to find it. In fact, the solution was probably something so simple and so mundane they would both have a good laugh over it—once they discovered what the heck it was.

Maybe a little snooping around after dinner tonight was in order. It was time to get serious about pitting his analytical mind against whatever forces were at work here. There were no mirrors in the hallway, but that painting might still provide a clue. He should also check out the study. If he could discover what the two locations had in common, he just might be able to piece the puzzle together.

"I'D LIKE TO DO a little investigating upstairs," Griff announced that evening. "By myself, if that's okay."

Nickie chuckled as she gazed fondly around the small parlor on the first floor where they sat relaxing after dinner. It was located at the back of the house off the kitchen, and included an odd, thrown-together mixture of priceless antiques and modern kitsch that appealed to the whimsical side of her nature. "Why should I object? Maybe this time you'll see him, too. I don't mind sharing.''

Griff shot her a disgruntled look before pushing himself out of his chair, a tacky recliner that had been poorly patched with matching brown tape along its fake leather armrests. ''I'd rather find out why *you're* seeing him.''

''Be my guest.''

Several minutes later she heard the faint sounds of the floor creaking over her head where Griff moved around upstairs. It sounded as if he was doing some serious hunting, but she knew he wouldn't find any evidence to prove the ghost was a figment of her imagination. She smiled at the thought that she couldn't apply that phrase to either of the new men in her life.

Half an hour passed before Griff returned downstairs. She suspected from the expression on his face that he hadn't uncovered anything significant. She knew it for certain when he threw himself down onto the recliner with a grunt of frustration.

''Well?'' she asked.

''Nothing.'' He frowned.

''I can't understand why he doesn't appear when you're around.'' Nickie bit her lip thoughtfully as she sat forward. ''Maybe you're just too unapproachable.''

''Is that so.'' He glared at her. ''If you're so all-fired approachable, why don't you go upstairs and see if he pops out of the woodwork while you're there?''

''He doesn't pop out of the woodwork,'' she protested. ''Besides, what will it prove if he does show himself to me again?''

"It will slam the door forever on a certain area of my inquiry."

She didn't like the sound of that, but doing something was better than just sitting around speculating, so she began disengaging herself from the loving embrace of her chair. "All right," she said in a dubious voice.

"Now what's the matter?"

"I don't know. It seems like entrapment or something, like we're trying to trick him into showing himself."

"There's nothing underhand about walking around in your own house, Nickie. If he wants to appear, he will, and if he doesn't, he won't." Griff groaned, throwing up his hands in disgust. "Listen to me. I'm talking as if this guy was a regular member of the family."

"I think he's becoming one," Nickie said cheerfully. "I sure wish I knew his name, though. It gets awfully irritating having to call him the 'ghost.'"

"I'm sure we'll all survive."

He followed her through the kitchen to the bottom of the stairs. "I'll wait right here. If you see him, call me."

She rolled her eyes at him but nodded.

She could feel his gaze on her back as she slowly climbed the stairs, her feet dragging. For some reason, this whole plan didn't sit well with her, although she couldn't find a reason for her uneasiness. She looked back over her shoulder and Griff nodded encouragingly, making a small shooing motion with his hand. She sighed and continued on.

She reached the landing between the floors where she had seen the dust cloud. Since the ghost had appeared, the dust hadn't given a repeat performance, causing her to think that maybe they were one and the same, that the swirling dust had been a warm-up.

By the time she reached the second floor her heartbeat had accelerated enough to let her know she was more nervous than she'd let on to Griff. She also felt like an idiot. It was one thing to stumble across him accidently, but to come looking for him on purpose made her feel foolish and awkward. Maybe she should just snap her fingers and call out, "Here ghost, nice ghost." She chuckled. Applying that nomenclature to the elegant gentleman with the wistful handsome face was becoming more difficult with each new encounter. She was beginning to think of him as more than just a collection of translucent particles.

He didn't appear to be around, she realized, relief flooding her as she wandered rather aimlessly through the hall. She turned to head back downstairs, but the thought of Griff waiting to greet her, a scowl on his face because she'd returned so quickly, not to mention with nothing to report, stopped her. She might as well make a quick circuit of all the rooms on this floor so she could say she had given it her all.

She strode briskly from door to door, feeling like the night watchman as she checked the Blue Salon and her bedroom, the small portrait gallery, the library and the Rose Room. Nothing. She was almost tempted to tell the ghost to make himself scarce, a notion as silly as calling out to him. He was a ghost, for heaven's sake. He wasn't in any danger from her or anyone else, not when he could just disappear like smoke in the wind.

Only one room remained to be checked—her study. She felt her throat tighten just before she peered reluctantly into its murky depths. After all, this was the last place she'd seen him. Since there was enough illumination from the hall lights, she didn't reach for the light switch. That seemed somehow sacrilegious.

At first she noticed nothing extraordinary as she glanced around the room. She had no intention of venturing any farther but remained at her post by the door, allowing her eyes to become adjusted to the rather gloomy interior. The wall on her left contained part of Bellefleur's library and was covered from floor to ceiling with rows of books. Many of the volumes were leather and the faint light that spilled across the floor glinted off the gilding on their spines. Her gaze continued to probe into the gloominess—and that's when she saw him, perched on the ladder that allowed one to reach the books on the uppermost shelves, his booted feet hooked over the rungs. Once again his back was to her.

She opened her mouth to call out to Griff, but she couldn't seem to break the spell the ghost's presence cast over her. He was obviously searching for a specific volume because he ran his forefinger along the spines, only pausing long enough to read each title before moving on. He appeared very solid in the shadowy darkness.

He didn't seem to realize she was standing there, and she felt as if she should say something to alert him to her presence. She supposed etiquette remained the same no matter what kind of being you were dealing with, but the thought of blurting out something like "Hello, would you mind telling me who you are and what you're doing here" brought a faint smile to her lips.

She was sure she hadn't said anything aloud, and yet the ghost must have heard something because he began turning slowly around. Either that or he had somehow sensed her presence. She found herself gripping the doorjamb with nervous fingers, bracing herself to meet his eyes.

He certainly was a courtly and chivalrous specter. He nodded politely and immediately began descending the ladder. Mustn't keep a lady waiting, Nickie thought with a repressed giggle. She hovered by the door in an agony of suspense, waiting for him to reach the floor, all thoughts of Griff pushed temporarily out of her mind. She couldn't have uttered a word now if her life had depended on it.

When he finally stepped off the bottom rung, he turned and bowed in her direction, his expressive movements graceful enough to suit the haughtiest queen. Nickie swallowed hard in a futile attempt to soothe her dry throat. She wasn't sure she could curtsy in return without falling on her face, so she simply nodded her head.

Suddenly his handsome chiseled lips lifted at the corners in a small smile and he tilted his head toward her, as though she had done something clever. He gestured, indicating himself and bowed again.

Was that something like "At your service"? By now she was beginning to feel a bit giddy, especially when she realized she was almost holding a conversation with a ghost, an apparition, a person who no longer dwelled among the living.

He watched her, his eyes filled with humor and patience. He was waiting for her to make the next move, but she had no idea what that might be.

"What do you want?" she whispered.

It came out in a croak quite unlike her normally soft voice, but the ghost didn't seem to notice or care as he again made a sweeping gesture with his hands. This time he pointed at her, his head cocked and his eloquent brows lifted to indicate a question.

He wanted to know who she was, Nickie realized in amazement. This was certainly a switch from all the ghostly protocol she had ever heard or read about. Well, what the heck. She shrugged and moistened her dry lips. "I'm Nickie, that is, Dominique DuPrés."

His smile was brilliant as he swept forward from the waist in the most extravagant and polished masculine bow he had yet bestowed on her. One arm moved briskly to a position across his stomach, while he tucked the other neatly behind his body. His tied-back hair fell forward over his shoulder because of the deepness of his salute. When he finally straightened, he was smiling in genuine ghostly pleasure, his eyes gleaming.

Nickie had never seen such expressive eyes. They looked very dark, although the feeble light was deceptive. He appeared to her in color and yet it was a faded sort of palette, like a bedspread that had once been a brilliant print but was now lovingly worn.

She didn't know what he needed from her, but she knew with a deep intuitive certainty that his visits had a purpose, and that she had a part to play in their resolution. She'd be happy if she could only help him smile more often and not be so melancholy, but she couldn't do anything until she knew who he was.

It was time to ask.

"Can you please tell me who you are?" This time her voice was strong and steady.

His entire countenance, even his posture, suddenly became wistful and sad as he gazed into space for several long moments. His expression reminded her of the time she'd spotted him in the window as a child. If she'd had her doubts before, they had completely vanished. This was the same individual she had seen then. And he was still melancholy after all these years. She longed to help him in whatever way she could.

"I know you can't talk, but can't you give me a clue?" she urged softly.

He cocked his head thoughtfully before bowing again in acquiescence. He was going to wear himself out with all that bowing, she thought, her mouth crooked in amusement.

"Nickie!" Griff shouted from downstairs. He sounded angry. "What are you doing up there?"

Nickie started guiltily. "Talking to the ghost," she called back. She felt like a regular hoyden, yelling her answer like that after all the courtliness and elegance that came so naturally to her companion.

She heard Griff's footsteps running up the stairs as she turned back to the ghost. He was shaking his head regretfully, one hand held out to her. "Don't go," she begged him. But he was already rapidly dissolving. By the time Griff burst into the room, there was nothing left but a few particles of dust.

"Where is he?" he barked.

"He's gone."

"Where was he?"

"Right here." She pointed sadly to the empty space in front of her. "He came down from the ladder where he was looking at the books."

Griff's head swiveled urgently as he looked from one corner to the other. He quickly searched the perimeter of the room, knocking against the paneling, feeling along the walls. Then he ran his hands up and down the ladder. Finally he crossed to the doorway and switched on the light. There was nothing to indicate anyone else had been there except Nickie.

"For some reason, you're not allowed to see him," she explained.

"Is that what he told you?" Griff snorted. "I suppose this time you held a conversation with him."

"He didn't actually speak any words, if that's what you mean. He doesn't talk. But when he gestures he has the most expressive face I've ever seen." Her gaze turned inward for a brief dreamy moment as she visualized the ghost's countenance. Then she focused again on Griff. "It's amazing how much body language can convey, isn't it?"

"Amazing." He bent closer, his gaze raking her face. "I'd appreciate it if you would wipe that infatuated lovesick expression off your face. He's gone."

She stared at him in amazement. "What in the world are you talking about?"

"You know damn well what I'm talking about."

"Are you implying that I'm falling for a ghost? Don't be ridiculous."

He didn't deign to reply, although he did mutter something succinct under his breath as he once again made a circuit of the room. *His* body language expressed puzzlement, annoyance and hardheaded determination.

She waited patiently, trying to see things as Griff did, with the eyes of a skeptic. One wall contained the large multipaned window, one wall the books. A giant landscape painting graced the third wall, and the desk sat against the remaining wall, on which hung several small paintings of flowers in heavy wooden frames gilded with gold paint.

"You're not going to find anything other than an ordinary room," she finally said, her tone gentle.

He swung his gaze to hers. "Do you wear glasses? Or contacts maybe?"

"Sorry. I have twenty-twenty vision."

"It figures. How did he leave this time?"

"Like before. He kept on dissolving until there were only a few particles left, and then they disappeared, too."

Griff blew out a breath, his eyes narrowed as they continued to probe the study.

"So. What's the answer?" she asked.

"There is no answer—yet," he added darkly. "I was hoping if the same thing happened in exactly the same spot, I'd know it had to be some kind of optical illusion."

"But he's not cooperating, is he?"

"Yeah, well, everything that happens can be filed under *E* for evidence. And I have been able to eliminate some options, even if they were pretty far out in the first place."

"Like what?"

"Like someone prowling around the place, disappearing into secret passages. There are no secret passages."

"That's a start," she agreed cheerfully. "If we keep going like this, maybe we can even boil it all down to the very real possibility that Bellefleur happens to harbor a ghost. Right now it's the simplest explanation. Why can't you accept it, take my word for it?"

"Because I'm a stubborn idiot who refuses to admit defeat." He sighed heavily. "Come on, let's go downstairs and you can fill me in on the rest."

"You're not going to like it," she told him teasingly.

"That's the understatement of the year."

She led the way down the staircase, past the interfloor landing and into the formal sitting room. She'd made a pact with herself to try to use all the rooms on a regular basis, and this one was next on her list.

The room could be considered a decorator's nightmare because, aside from the major grouping of furniture, nothing matched. The couch and two chairs were of mahogany in a style called French Victorian. They were mounted on incongruously slender cabriole legs with whorled feet. In the center of the imposing trio stood a marble table whose cartouche-shaped surface was carved with a motif of roses and whose legs sported scroll carvings. The walls held an assortment of grim portraits and gloomy landscapes, obviously rejects from the rest of the lighter, more rococo art found throughout the rest of the house. They probably needed to be cleaned—she would have to see to it.

It was not a cozy room by any means, but it seemed as good a place as any to discuss a ghost.

Griff threw himself into one of the balloon-backed chairs.

"Are you a brandy connoisseur?" she asked him with a small smile. "I opened one of the dusty bottles I found in the wine cellar, and it's quite excellent."

"Sounds good," he replied in a tone that indicated at this point he was willing to settle for Tennessee rotgut.

"Two brandies coming right up."

"And quit sounding so damned cheerful," he added.

She grinned at him before she turned and hurried to the kitchen.

Minutes later she was back, handing him a brandy snifter. She settled herself into one stiff, brocade-covered corner of the couch, setting her glass carefully on the marble-topped table to avoid the rose decorations. She was sure its surface had experienced harder wear in its long life, but she wasn't about to add to it.

She glanced at Griff, who was sitting at an angle in his chair, his eyes closed as he gratefully inhaled brandy fumes. They must have cleared his head, for when he opened his eyes they looked like chips of green bottle glass, hard and sharp with intelligence.

"So, tell me."

She proceeded to explain the details of her interlude, including her reactions. Subjective though they were, they remained the core of what she'd experienced, because most of her interaction with the ghost hadn't consisted of words but of silent implications and broad hand gestures.

"You mean this...this ghost asked you who you were?"

"Not in so many words of course. But he seemed pleased when I told him. I'm sure he was just about to provide me with a clue to his own identity when a certain party came thundering up the stairs like the charge of the Light Brigade and he was forced to disappear."

"What do you mean, forced? I never said he had to leave."

"Well, he obviously felt differently." She raised her eyebrows expressively. "Of course, that's just my personal interpretation of events, but since I was the only one present, you'll have to forgo a second opinion."

There was a long silence while he digested everything. He wasn't frowning exactly, but the wrinkle between his eyebrows indicated he wasn't particularly enjoying himself.

He leaned forward in his seat, pinning her with his hard green gaze. "There's one question you haven't answered to my satisfaction."

"What's that?" she asked, smiling congenially.

"Why didn't you call me sooner?"

Her smile fled. "I...I don't know. I was spellbound, I guess, and one thing led to another."

"This is not the way to convince me about what you're seeing."

"I suppose not."

"It's also very convenient that your ghost doesn't want me to see him. At least according to you."

Nickie bristled at the implication. She'd never claimed to understand the ghost's motivations. "Maybe he's a family-only spook," she retorted.

"Do you have a boyfriend back East?"

"What?" She frowned at his question, but one look at his stern expression told her it would be easier to answer than try to argue about why he wanted to know. She'd find out soon enough. "No."

"Have you recently broken up with someone?"

"No. Well, sort of, but it was a friendly parting. Our relationship wasn't exactly setting the world on fire. What are you getting at?"

"Nothing."

"Yes, you are." She eyed him suspiciously as the light dawned. "Are we back to that again? Listen, I am not falling for him. I simply like him. He happens to be a very likable ghost. Maybe you're lucky you haven't seen him, because if you did, you'd like him and want to help him, too."

"Help him do what?"

"I wish I knew. But he wants something, that's evident."

"Maybe he wants you."

"Don't be silly." She grinned, trying to visualize such a scenario. "I can see the headlines in one of those scandal rags now—Tennessee Woman in Torrid Relationship with Ancestral Ghost." She picked up her brandy and took a small sip. "I don't think it would work out very well. After all, you can't make love with a ghost."

"How do you know? Have you tried?"

"Don't be ridiculous."

"But you're curious."

She groaned and rolled her eyes in amused frustration. "I don't know which is worse—being suspected of fabricating a ghost or being accused of desiring kinky sex with him. Thanks all the same, but I think I'll stick to the kind of men who don't disintegrate into thin air. Although," she added with a judicious chuckle, "I suppose some of them wish they could do just that when the going gets rough."

"This guy may disappear, but he keeps coming back for more," Griff pointed out.

It was a flat statement and Nickie didn't like the sound of it. "So?"

He shrugged. "It's just a simple observation."

"Maybe if we find out what he wants and give it to him, he'll go away completely."

"That depends on what he wants."

"Oh, right. According to you, he wants me." She tilted her head in amused consideration. "Well, why not? He's charming and handsome. And thoughtful—remember the flowers for which you've offered no other explanation. All in all, he's the perfect lover."

But Griff wasn't laughing along with her. "Don't forget I've seen the expression on your face when you talk about him."

"Get serious. He's a ghost, for heaven's sake. Of course I look strange when I mention him."

"I *am* serious." Something in his voice caused her to meet his gaze, and what she saw there made her throat constrict.

But it was his next words that really set her heart racing. "If it's a lover you're looking for, I'd be happy to volunteer for the position."

# Chapter Six

She stared at him, her mouth open in amazement. No words came out because she had no idea what to say in response to his astonishing offer. Instead, she watched him as he rose from his seat and walked around the marble-topped table to hunker down in front of her, taking her hands into the engulfing heat of his callused palms. She had to admit he was as compelling as any ghost and a darned sight warmer.

"I may not be as romantic as he is, but I think I could do a better job of keeping you satisfied."

"Is that what you think all this is, a plot to maneuver you into bed with me?" she demanded, finding her voice to defend herself even though he hadn't exactly charged her with anything. At the moment it was easier than admitting how much she liked the idea of making love with Griffin McInnis.

He rose to a standing position, tugging her to her feet and sliding his arms around her waist. "Judging from your reaction, obviously not."

That reply mollified her enough so that when he bent to brush his warm mouth against hers, she didn't pull away.

"But even if that had been the case," he murmured, "I wouldn't have minded the idea that a woman wanted me enough to resort to such a plan." He lifted his hand so that he could cup her chin. "In your case, all you had to do was ask."

His voice was a husky whisper as his lips covered hers in an openmouthed kiss, something she realized she had been wanting since the first time he'd kissed her. It didn't matter that he was only a temporary addition to her life. Even his opinion about the ghost didn't matter. She couldn't have refused him if her life had depended on it.

His hand was warm against her throat. When he slid it around to the back of her head, spearing his fingers into her hair, it was all she could do not to moan aloud at the pleasurable sensations coursing along her neck and shoulders. She knew she should stop him now before this went any further, but vaguely she realized that another few minutes wouldn't cause any more harm than had already been done. He immediately sensed her hesitation and pressed the advantage of her captivity, using his hand to steady her head and using his lips to part hers so he could kiss her even more deeply and intimately. By the time he withdrew, they were both breathless.

"I think maybe we should just agree to disagree about the ghost," he said. "Obviously there are other areas where we're more in accord."

His words sobered her into pulling away. She wondered if he thought of her as the sort of gullible female who could be sweet-talked into having an affair with him. The gullible label certainly didn't apply to her, but she couldn't argue with the powerful persuasion of the rest of the equation. She realized that if he hung in there just a while longer, he would probably be able to sweep her off her feet and into his bed. All her defenses were down due to a combination of unusual factors, including the ghost whose presence he so adamantly refused to countenance.

There was no doubt about the attraction and the chemistry between them. But it certainly put a damper on things when the man who held you in his arms didn't trust you enough to believe in you. Of course she realized it was asking a lot of any mortal to expect him to automatically accept the existence of a supernatural phenomenon not witnessed with his own eyes. She wondered how easily *she* would believe him if the shoe were on the other foot. She thought she'd be inclined to take his word; if nothing else, she would certainly reserve her judgment until all the facts were in.

She gazed up at him. His eyes reflected the spark they'd ignited between them, and his desire was evident in the glittering green fire that smoldered in their depths. He obviously was able to put aside his investigations into the ghost in favor of more immediate gratification.

"I don't think this is such a good idea," she said softly, raising her hands to his shoulders in an effort to keep some distance between them as he again began bending toward her.

He stopped. "Why not?" He reached up to brush a wayward lock of hair back from her temple.

She shrugged. "Lots of reasons. Two in particular."

"Name them."

"For one thing, you don't believe me about the ghost."

His arms tightened momentarily, but he didn't release her right away. "To be quite honest, I don't know what to think anymore. All this goes against everything I've ever been taught to believe, along with everything I've been trained to do." He dropped his arms from around her waist, stepping back and shoving his hands into his pockets. "I work with the laws of physics to make sure that structures remain standing a long, long time. Everything I do can be proved with an equation. It's hard to break away from that kind of thinking. What's the second reason?"

"You'll be leaving soon."

He nodded, his expression suddenly wary even though his voice remained carefully neutral. "I have to be on my next job in a week."

"Right, seven days. We'll barely have time to solve the mystery of the ghost in that short amount of time, never mind anything else."

"At the moment I don't seem to give a damn about the ghost or anything else."

"Well, someone has to. Especially since he doesn't seem to be inclined to leave us alone."

"Just because I'm leaving doesn't mean we can't continue to see each other."

She shuddered at the thought of being his part-time, long-distance lover. It was all too easy to visualize herself drifting aimlessly from room to beautiful room in Bellefleur, waiting for his calls and yearning desperately for the occasional visit.

"I don't like to start things that have a predetermined ending already built-in." She held up her hand to forestall him when he started to speak. "Believe me, I know what I'm talking about here. You'd promise to phone and visit, and at the time you'd really mean it. But once the ties of friendship and affection are severed by distance, it's never the same. I've been through that scene too many times in my life not to know exactly how it will turn out."

"So what are you going to do? Lock up your heart and throw away the key?"

She shrugged carelessly even as a sudden pain shot through her body at the image he'd conjured up. She could suddenly see herself as a lonely old woman just like her great-aunt obsessively dedicated to Bellefleur because she had nothing else in her life to call her own. "I'm just being practical," she insisted.

"Practical, oh sure," he said, slanting her an amused disbelieving glance. "After everything that's already happened, I'd say any chance either of us had at practicality has been shot to hell." His expression sobered. "I know my job takes me all over the country. I haven't been settled since I left my parents' home to go to college. So what am I supposed to do? Give up the work I love so I can roost in one spot long enough that a woman will have me? Or maybe I should retire altogether from the playing field of relationships and just resign myself to spending the rest of my life alone."

"I was only referring to my own conduct. I certainly wasn't trying to tell you how to run your life."

"Weren't you?"

"No, of course not. I'm sorry if it came out sounding that way." His insistence on deliberately misreading her intentions was making her feel both cornered and angry. After all, she was only one lone female, and she was sure there were plenty of other women who would leap at the chance to see where fate and Griff would lead them.

"I happen to like moving around," he explained carefully. "I like to see new places, experience new things, take on new challenges. There's nothing wrong with that, and there's nothing wrong with wanting someone in my life, even if I don't know where I'm going to be from one month to the next, or how things will turn out."

"How convenient for you," she said tartly. "It sounds like you need to find a woman who likes to travel around as much as you do."

"And we both know that you've found your roots here at Bellefleur." He ran a disgruntled hand through his hair. "Look, you're right. I know you're trying to stabilize your life and I'm just a vagabond passing through on my way to someplace else."

He took another step back from her, and Nickie felt an unwanted stab of rejection beneath her anger at his typically male attitude. She ran her fingers along the back of the antique sofa, a smile pasted on her face even as her throat tightened with conflicting emotions.

She wished she could allow herself to live for the moment, but she knew it would only result in pain and heartbreak later on. She had made a solemn vow that she was never going to move again, that she was going to put down permanent roots now that she'd found the perfect location. But as she gazed at Griff's handsome, brooding face she almost believed it might be worth it to set that pledge aside.

She gave herself a mental shake. It was time to return to the reality of her life as she'd chosen to mold it. She was already in deeper with Griff than she'd ever intended to be; extricating herself was going to be hard enough without creating more physical and emotional ties to bind them together. No, she assured herself with a heavy heart, she was doing the right thing, taking the only possible course of action.

"I'll tell you what," Griff said, interrupting her ruminations. "Since we've already agreed to disagree about the ghost, we can use the same tactic here."

She sat back down on the couch and reached for her brandy, taking a long swallow before speaking. "All right. Does this mean you're going to abandon your investigation?"

"It means I'm going to redouble my efforts." He smiled at her reassuringly as he lowered himself into his seat, his careful movements unconsciously respectful of the age and rather unsubstantial contours of the oddly shaped piece of furniture. In spite of his efforts, the delicate framework still gave a small squeak of protest. "Once I finally do expose what's behind these ghostly visitations, who knows what will happen?"

"Nothing will happen. There's a limit to gratitude, you know."

He just grinned as he leaned forward, pinning her with his intense gaze. "I'm going to blow this thing wide open. It's time someone really got busy and compiled every scrap of detail connected with this entire setup. That would include anything that's ever been said or written about the ghost, and everyone who's ever come in contact with him, whether personally or through hearsay." He polished off his brandy, then stared at the snifter with obvious appreciation. "Did your great-aunt keep a diary? Or records of the estate?"

"I don't know, but I can check."

"Good. We'll need to find out about the history of this house, who built it, when and why…"

"There are probably books in the second-floor library that contain that sort of information."

"Great."

He continued to cradle the empty snifter in his hands, rolling the glass between his palms in a way that made her long to feel them caressing her. She thrust the thought from her mind, forcing her attention back to the point. "There's always the Linton Historical Society," she added with a smile, remembering Marie-Claire's irrational feud with them.

She could see that his brain was racing a mile a minute now that he had something to wrap his intellect around. She realized he had truly meant what he'd said about taking on challenges. He didn't reveal his restless nature outwardly, but she thought she understood better why he needed to move on.

She sighed when she realized she could have been the one to fill up his spare time while he tended to the garden. He was intense in his involvement until he solved whatever he put his attention to and then she supposed it was over. Still, the idea of being the focus of his thoughts was compelling and more than a little alluring. She was going to have to be careful not to fall into that trap.

"I've been approaching this from the wrong angle all along," he continued, slapping his hand against his thigh for emphasis. "I've been working in the dark, trying to explain a phenomenon without any sense of its background history. That's like trying to build a bridge from scratch without using the data every previous engineer has compiled about structure and stress and tension."

She didn't know what to say, so she just nodded in agreement. Even though she'd longed for this very thing to happen, now she wasn't sure if she liked the idea of Griff's working wholeheartedly on solving the mystery of the ghost. She had the irrational fear that his laser attention, laced as it was with so much skepticism, might cause her visitor to disappear forever. She didn't want that, not when she was closer to finding out why he had materialized in her home in the first place.

Still, it would be nice to be working alongside the formidable Griffin McInnis for a change, instead of tagging along behind him as she had that long-ago summer. She wondered how long their truce about searching for the origins of the ghost would last. Probably until the first piece of evidence that supported her theory came to light, she thought with a rueful little smile. It was only too obvious that their unique interpretations of whatever "facts" they managed to uncover were on a collision course.

"So, where do we start?" she inquired politely.

"My grandfather is a key player in all this. We'll go visit him in Memphis tomorrow afternoon."

"It won't upset him to talk about this subject?"

"Upset him? Are you kidding? You're going to have to be careful he doesn't talk your ear off."

THE NEXT MORNING Griff made sure he was out of the house before Nickie could even think of rolling out of bed. The first rays of the sun peeking above the horizon found him already in the garden, his wheelbarrow filled with rakes and hoes and hedge clippers, ready to buckle down to work. Besides, if he wanted to take time away from refurbishing the garden to visit his grandfather this afternoon, he needed to get a head start.

He grabbed the clippers and began to trim the trees along the main walkway that led to the fountain, chuckling as he recalled his life-changing experience in Bellefleur's version of a bathroom earlier that morning. No matter how many times he went in there, its size still shocked him. The room was as big as the studio apartment he had rented while on that job in Toronto. The bathtub sat on a raised platform behind a beautiful hand-painted screen that depicted a ballroom scene, complete with ladies in long diaphanous gowns whirling gracefully in the arms of gentlemen in evening clothes. The old-fashioned claw feet of the tub were edged in gold that curled up the curving sides of white porcelain in a scroll-like pattern. Anyone who actually tried to fill the tub to the top would probably lower Linton's water reserves by a foot. A person could learn the backstroke in its cavernous depths.

His mind wouldn't let him stray for long from the matter that had really been bothering him. He was in turmoil. Somehow the ghost and the garden and his desire for Nickie had become jumbled in his mind like a tossed salad. He'd finally found himself offering to dig to the bottom of things for his own sanity and peace of mind. He would help her discover who this ghost was. He didn't care whether the ghost was real anymore; *Nickie's* presence was real enough to counter everything else. Since he had to stay here and finish the gardens for his grandfather, any sort of puzzle to solve would help distract him from the desire to wrap his arms around Nickie's slender body and kiss her senseless. Whether it would work or not was anybody's guess.

It seemed as if he'd been working only a short time when he heard approaching footsteps. When he looked back over his shoulder he saw Nickie rounding the corner, a cup of coffee in one hand and a doughnut in the other. He hadn't eaten anything in his hurry to leave the house, and the sight made his mouth water. His stomach had been growling since he'd begun work.

"What time is it?" he asked as she drew nearer.

"Almost ten. Either you're very neat and did all your dishes and cleaned out the coffeemaker after using it, or you didn't have anything to eat or drink this morning."

She held out the cup and he took it gratefully. He nodded at the doughnut. "Is that up for grabs, as well?"

"Be my guest. I've already had one."

"Thanks." He took a bite, leaving half the doughnut remaining. "Hey, this is good. It's not from the supermarket, is it?"

"No. Linton now boasts its very own bakery. It's only open until noon, but they know what's important because it has a drive-through window."

Griff polished off the doughnut with his third bite, washing it down with another swallow of coffee. "So, did you see him this morning?"

She almost looked embarrassed. "Yes, actually, I did." She glanced away for a moment, and Griff had to grit his teeth against the soft, slightly bewildered expression stealing over her face. The bewilderment didn't bother him, but that limpid gleam that made the brown of her eyes darken with indulgence was really starting to get to him.

"And?" He tried not to sound impatient, but he was thinking he would like to get his hands on the guy, just once.

"He was walking along the hallway, apparently on his way to the back of the house." She bit her lip. "When he saw me he stopped and held out what he'd been carrying so I could see it better."

"Well, what was it?"

She glanced away. "A sketchbook."

"A sketchbook?" Of all the things he had expected her to say, this hadn't even made the list.

"At first I thought it was mine, you know, from my desk." She shook her head. "It wasn't."

He stared at her as she stood there, lost in thought. The moment went on for so long that he was finally forced to speak to bring her back to the present. Otherwise, she might have remained mooning over the ghost the rest of the morning. "Then what happened?" he asked. He couldn't completely keep the testiness from his voice. "Did he offer to draw your picture?"

She looked at him in faint surprise. "No, of course not. He simply turned and continued down the hall.

But from the way he held the book under his arm, I could see that the top sketch was a back view of Bellefleur, probably drawn from that first bench along the walkway. I could see part of the fountain in the foreground."

He heard the slight catch in her voice. "So?"

"So if he sketched the house from that bench, that means he's able to go outside. I thought ghosts were supposed to stay in their houses."

"Haven't you noticed? Your ghost doesn't seem to be following any of the rules." His eyes narrowed thoughtfully as he blew out an exasperated breath. "Did he continue walking away from you?"

"Yes. When he reached the end of the hall, he turned and gave me one of those elegant little bows of his, and then he began dissolving into thin air again, strolling right into the Rose Room at the same time. I immediately ran into the study, but my own sketchbook was on the desk right where I'd left it."

"Great." Griff stared down at his now empty coffee cup in disgust. "If nothing else, we're getting a solid lesson on what a ghost does with his spare time."

"Do you think maybe he was an artist? That he painted some of the pictures hanging on the walls around here?"

"Maybe," Griff replied as neutrally as he could manage under the circumstances. It was more likely the damned spook was trying to weasel his way into Nickie's good graces, knowing she was an artist herself. It was what *he* would do if he were a ghost trying to impress a mortal.

He quickly shook his head to clear it of such crazy speculations. This whole business was becoming more impossible with every dawning day. He couldn't believe the things he was saying and doing; his life was becoming like some crazy dream, "Twin Peaks" in action. Every morning found him further and further from the world of rational thinking and normal living. Thank goodness none of his engineering friends could see him calmly discussing a ghost who carried a sketchbook and showed definite artistic leanings.

"From what I could see, it was beautiful work," Nickie continued wistfully, her eyes inwardly focused to better visualize the drawing in question. "He must have been quite an artist."

"I suppose that's as good a place as any for you to start," he informed her briskly. He had promised himself to allow Nickie to research the identity of the ghost, no matter how far off course it might take her, and he intended to stick to that pledge. "You can check the signatures on all the paintings in the house, see if anything useful turns up."

"Good idea," she said. Her eyes glowed with excitement. "What time are we leaving for Memphis?"

"Let's say around five. I should be able to finish tidying up this quadrant by then. We can also get something to eat on the way."

"Fine. Are you done with that?" she asked pointing at his cup. When he nodded, she took it from his hand and whirled around, walking quickly and gracefully back the way she'd come. She was obviously excited to get started now that she had a direction to take. There was going to be no stopping her, he decided ruefully, as he watched her disappear around the corner where a statue of a pair of gracefully entwined wood nymphs stood.

Now that he thought about it, she reminded him of a nymph herself with her slender, supple dancer's body and her graceful ways. He wanted her as he hadn't wanted a woman in a long time. He was more married to his job than perhaps a man should be, but Nickie had a way of making him forget all that. He knew she was probably correct about trying to conduct a long-distance affair; it made no sense to start something so risky, but in Nickie's case he found himself inclined to make an exception.

As he reached for the clippers, he realized he hadn't been involved with a woman for a long time. He ran it through his mind and discovered that his last relationship had been over a year ago. There simply hadn't been time with his busy schedule, and in any case, there hadn't been anyone he'd cared to get involved with.

He thrust the clipper blades around the protruding branch of a maple tree, feeling the satisfying snap of the limb and watching its intertwined leaves catch with their fellows for a moment before it tumbled to the walkway in front of him. He supposed Nickie was right; he should find someone who leaned more toward footloose and fancy-free. He certainly should refrain from interfering with someone who had painstakingly decided on a permanent establishment.

And yet he couldn't seem to help wanting her—a foolish state of mind no matter how you looked at it. Not only did she insist on staying put, she had the strongest reason to do so, namely Bellefleur. Anyone would think working in these magnificent gardens would serve to remind him just who owned what around here.

It was a dilemma, all right, and one that held no immediate answers. This burning desire, which seemed to crash like an ocean wave over his willpower and his common sense, was capable of sweeping all objections aside. He assured himself that he could control it, that he was master of his fate and his emotions. The best solution remained the one he was already following—keep working on getting the gardens ready for his grandfather to visit and use his spare time to solve the mystery of Nickie's ghost. However, to his way of thinking, his feelings for her were more dangerous than any ghost could ever be. In any event, he ought to be able to stay out of trouble for the six days remaining until he left for California.

As for Nickie, he would use her as a foil for testing the theories he came up with on whatever it was she was seeing. He would keep his attention focused strictly on the puzzle he'd promised to solve, never forgetting for a second who he was or where he was going. He could only hope for both their sakes that his feelings for her would fade into something more manageable.

They always had before.

## Chapter Seven

When Nickie came tripping downstairs at four-fifty-five, she found Griff already waiting in his car, a small sporty American model in shades of silvery green. He had parked it near the edge of the house under an ancient oak tree whose mighty limbs towered over the roof of the attic. Her eyes followed the line of its massive trunk as she recalled the time Marie-Claire had informed her that this particular tree had been planted when the house was first built. She'd tried very hard at the time to picture it as a tiny sapling, but her child's mind found it impossible. It was simply too big and too magnificent.

"Hi," she said cheerfully as she ducked her head to peer inside.

She thought she would grow used to the greenness of his eyes, but it was still a shock when he lifted his gaze from what looked like an architectural magazine to meet hers. "Hi." He smiled. "You look awfully pleased about something."

She grinned back. "I am. I've decided this place must be good for my creative muse."

"Oh?"

"I've never done such quality work so effortlessly. It's incredible. I swear my hand knows exactly what it wants to do without my telling it anything. It just moves across the paper smoothly and effortlessly."

"It must be the company you've been keeping."

"Are you referring to yourself or the ghost?" she inquired teasingly.

He reached across to unlock the passenger door. "Myself, of course. But speaking of the ghost, hop in and tell me what you've discovered about your artist friend this afternoon."

She slanted him a narrow look as she opened the door and slid into the passenger seat. He sounded suspiciously unconcerned about the subject of the supernatural, something that usually openly exasperated him, but she wasn't about to question it or complain.

"I've decided we must give him a name."

Griff grinned and started the engine. "I'll leave that privilege to you."

"All right. We can't call him Bob or Ted or anything prosaic. If he's an artist, he needs a good solid artist's name."

"How about Picasso? Van Gogh? Rembrandt?"

She laughed. "No, those names are already taken. Besides, his style is uniquely his own."

"Then what do you suggest?" He let out the clutch as he shifted into first gear. The car's engine sounded more like a purring tiger than a man-made compilation of cylinders, valves and pistons.

"I thought maybe something simple like Charles or Louis or Henri."

"You think the ghost is French?"

"It seems a likely possibility that he's either French or of French descent, don't you think? Everything else about Bellefleur is French, right down to the name." She tucked her purse beside her leg. "There was something about the way he used his hands, not to mention those expressive eyes and his dark good looks."

"Let's not go into all that again," Griff muttered. "Just pick something."

"All right, Charles it is."

"Can I call him Chuck for short?" He didn't look at her, but she knew his eyes were gleaming with amusement as he accelerated smoothly down the street. Through every gear change, the car continued to hum like a champion.

"Don't even think about it," she retorted. "By the way, who does your tune-ups?"

"I do."

"Oh. Nice job."

It figured, she thought with a small chuckle as they quickly reached the edge of town and the two-lane road that would take them to the highway to Memphis. Anything Griff turned his hand to was bound to come out as close to perfect as a human could possibly get. She had already seen the evidence of what happened when he turned his laser attention to a task. Just look at what he'd already accomplished with the front section of the gardens: the hedges were now trimmed back into their original geometric shapes, the walkway was perfectly edged and swept, the flower beds weeded and in some cases replanted. The bridges he worked on would probably outlast the pyramids. And his kisses were nothing to sneeze at, either.

That last thought brought her up short, reminding her that it was time to head for safer ground. "I did a preliminary check of signatures on the paintings, but it wasn't very successful."

"Why not?"

She threw him a dispirited glance before settling back against the supple leather seat. "You know how it is—half the time the artist used his initials or some anagram of his name and the other half you can't make heads or tails of it. I recognized a few of the names, so I checked out their likenesses in one of my art books. But none of them was him—Charles, I mean."

"It wouldn't be much of a mystery if you could solve it on the first try."

"Somehow that doesn't comfort me."

He chuckled. "Don't worry. My grandfather will set you straight."

"Why are you suddenly so cheerful about dragging your grandfather into all this, when the other night in the garden you avoided the subject like the plague?"

"I came to the conclusion it might do him good to talk with you."

"Why?"

Griff shrugged, but she wasn't fooled for a minute by his casual pose. "Just a hunch. You can tell him how the garden is coming along, for one thing. That should make him happy."

"I'd be glad to tell him. You're doing a wonderful job," she said and meant it. "But that's not the only reason, is it."

"No, that's not the only reason." He glanced over at her for a moment before returning his eyes to the road. "I never said that my grandfather was reluctant to speak about the ghost, only that I was reluctant to hear about it. He'll be thrilled to know you've seen him. I'm hoping it will boost his spirits enough to help speed his recovery."

"It's nice to know Charles is good for something besides his elegant presence," she said with a theatrical sigh. Then she grinned. "It'll also be nice to have someone believe me for a change."

He declined to comment on her teasingly pointed statement, instead using that precise moment to pass a car he'd been following without a sign of hurry or impatience for the past fifteen minutes. The traffic had thickened considerably as they entered the suburbs, and in the distance she could see some of the taller buildings of Memphis. She turned to watch the scenery through the window.

Forty-five minutes later, after a quick hamburger, they pulled into the driveway of a modern ranch-style house. The entire neighborhood was new, and the shrubbery surrounding each dwelling looked sparse and small. Nickie could never understand why they chopped down all the tall trees when they built these developments. It only forced the residents to start all over with saplings that would take half a lifetime to establish themselves.

"It doesn't look as though my sister's home," Griff said as they climbed the steps to the front door. "She probably ran out to the store or something. Come on."

"Didn't you tell her you were coming?"

"No. She would only have spent the day worrying about what to feed us for dinner, and then spent a fortune trying to provide me with steak and all my other favorite foods.''

He pushed opened the front door and they entered the air-conditioned interior. The furnishings were as sparse as the landscaping outside, with only a small decorative table and matching mirror visible in the foyer. There wasn't a single piece of art on the freshly painted walls. In fact, the only spot of color was a reflection from the green-and-gold glass of the small decorative window beside the door.

"Tracy and Jack only moved in here last year, and with Jack trying to start up a business, there hasn't been a lot left over for anything nonessential,'' Griff explained, then gestured. "My grandfather's room is this way.''

She followed him up the carpeted stairs. The place still carried the unmistakable smell of sawdust, plaster and paint. Her sandals sank into the thick pile of the tan wall-to-wall carpeting of the hallway.

"Granddad?''

"That you, Griff?'' The raspy voice that called out was filled with delight.

"Yeah,'' Griff replied as he turned the corner into the far bedroom. He gestured Nickie inside. "I've brought you a visitor.''

Nickie gazed curiously at the man in the bed. He didn't look much like Griff, but he also wasn't the way she remembered him from her childhood. She visualized a stocky man with big arms and shoulders. Even lying down as he was, she could see that his once robust frame was wasted. The shock of hair that she remembered tumbling over his brow was now white, although it still showed traces of the dark brown it had once been. His face was tanned and yet looked pale underneath. The skin of his face and neck was loose as if he'd recently lost a good deal of weight.

He broke into a warm grin at the sight of her, and the way his mouth tilted up at the corners was so instantly familiar it stirred memories of the man he had once been. She couldn't help but smile in return.

"This is Nickie DuPrés, Marie-Claire's grand-niece."

"I know who she is, Griff my boy, I've got two eyes in my head." The old man turned to her and held out a large tanned hand, which he used to give hers a squeeze. There was still a lot of power in those strong fingers. "You grew up to be just as pretty as I always predicted," he said with a twinkle in his eye. "It's a pleasure to see you again after all these years."

"You, too, Mr. McInnis."

"Call me Harry, sweetheart. The other sounds too formal, and I'm not a formal man."

She smiled. "All right."

"Have a seat." He gestured toward a couple of chairs that sat at the side and foot of the bed. In spite of the age and illness that had ravaged his body, his spirits seemed in working order. She could identify no sign of depression, although that didn't mean it wasn't there.

"Well, this is a surprise," the old man continued, his tone still jovial. "Why didn't you call ahead? I thought your sister and Jack needed a break from trying to entertain me, so I sent them off to the movies." His eyes narrowed in shrewd speculation on his grandson. "Don't tell me you've finished with the gardens."

"Not yet, Granddad."

"But they already look beautiful," Nickie put in eagerly. "Griff has cleared off the main walkway and clipped the box yews and replanted the flower beds. Your gardens are magnificent, a work of art."

The old man's faded blue eyes glowed with pride. "Thank you, lass." He leaned forward to grasp her hand, his voice a loud stage whisper as he continued, "I know my grandson thinks Marie-Claire DuPrés was a snooty old biddy and a tyrant to boot, but she gave me the opportunity to push the talent God gave me to the limit to create those gardens, and I'll never say a bad word about her."

"I understand," Nickie said soothingly.

"Those years were the most magical time of my life," he said, shaking his head reminiscently. His free hand plucked at the cover, and Nickie realized how hard it must be for an outdoor man like Harry Mc-Innis to stay in bed. "I can't explain it, but from the minute Mademoiselle DuPrés—she liked me to use the French form of address even though I usually butchered the accent. Anyway, like I was saying, from the minute she told me what she wanted to do, it was as if the project was born under a lucky star. Everything about it went right. Everything went smoothly. It was the darnedest thing you ever saw."

Nickie nodded encouragingly. Harry leaned even closer, although he didn't lower his voice to match the intimate gesture. He obviously had something to get off his chest. His dramatic posturing seemed aimed at impressing Griff as much as anything else, because he glanced at his grandson almost defiantly before he continued, "She always swore it was because of the ghost she'd seen—the ghost of Bellefleur."

Nickie's eyes widened and she couldn't help glancing at Griff, either. His head was slightly cocked in a listening position, but otherwise he gave no indication that what he'd just heard might be upsetting in any fashion. In fact his face was like a stone mask, albeit a pleasant one.

If she was surprised at his calm reaction, the next words out of his mouth were a total shock. "Nickie's seen the ghost herself, Granddad," he announced as though giving the daily weather report. "He's been roaming around the halls on a regular basis practically since the day she arrived."

Harry's eyes lit up in what Nickie could only describe as exultation. He turned to her with a broad smile. "I knew he'd come back." He pointed a knowing finger at Griff. "That's because you're fixing up the gardens. Didn't I tell you he wanted it? Didn't I tell you?"

"You told me," Griff agreed.

"This is wonderful," the old man said happily. "Just wonderful."

Nickie couldn't believe the change that had come over him at the news. Harry's cheeks had acquired color and his face seemed to have filled out before her very eyes. He was even sitting up straighter, and his shoulders were now thrown back, instead of hunched forward. She glanced shrewdly at Griff. He must have known that his grandfather would react like this and figured desperate times called for desperate measures, even if it meant discussing apparitions.

"He's a very special ghost, you know," Harry explained, a devilish twinkle suddenly sparkling in the depths of his eyes. It made them look like pale blue sapphires. "I hope you gave him a proper curtsy."

"I thought about it," she said with a reminiscent chuckle. "At the time I was too stunned to do more than nod my head."

"In case you didn't know, that was the king of France you were gawking at," he added softly. He gazed innocently into the distance as though his revelation wasn't a shock to his listeners.

"The king of France!" Both Nickie and Griff spoke at the same time.

"Oh, my goodness," she added reverently. She frowned as she recalled every detail of Charles's appearance. As aristocratic as he had been, he hadn't looked like a picture of any king of France she'd ever seen. Unless she was seeing him in his youth, before he got too kingly and regal. "Which one?"

"To be honest with you, I can't say for certain. Marie-Claire told me one time, but I could never remember. It was a French name with a number after it—you know how all those kings sound alike. Not that I ever saw him myself, mind," he added in a confidential whisper.

"Didn't my aunt ever describe what he looked like?"

"No, and I never asked. I just figured he ran around in a big ermine cape with a crown on his head. How else would she know it was a king?"

"How indeed," Griff interjected wryly. "Granddad, just because the woman who told you there was a ghost running around loose happened to be your employer is no reason to believe her out of hand. Why did you?"

"I'm impressed that you're taking all this so calm and rational-like, Griff." Harry winked at Nickie. Obviously he wasn't about to let anything dampen his high spirits. "What did you do, lass? Cast a spell over him?"

Nickie shrugged and laughed. "We've been over the same ground so many times I think I've just worn him down."

"To answer my grandson's question, I'd better start from the beginning." He settled himself more comfortably against the pillows. "I've never been one to scoff at the unexplainable. There's more to this world than any of us will ever know while we're here. Besides, what's the harm in letting people have their illusions if it makes them happy? So, when she first told me, I simply shrugged and took her at her word."

He nodded at Nickie. "Your great-aunt was the most practical, no-nonsense person to walk this earth. She might have been hard to get along with, but that's because she was so forthright. She always said exactly what she meant and told you exactly how she felt. And the thing she was proudest of was her French ancestry."

"I can vouch for that," Nickie said.

"It all started right after that last time you visited her, young lady. The very next week she drove to Memphis to see Jean Haversoll, a well-known expert on French history who teaches at the university. After she returned she told me that she wanted to construct a garden. She said it was for the ghost. She insisted he was tired of being cooped up in the house and wanted to be able to go outside."

"Oh, my." Nickie felt a shiver go down her spine. "She really did listen to what I was trying to tell her. After I saw him in the window, I couldn't get the idea out of my head that he was sad because he couldn't go outside. I didn't know at the time that he was a ghost."

Harry nodded thoughtfully. "I suspected you'd done something to instigate things. It wasn't long afterward that she began talking about leaving you the house."

Nickie started. "You mean she left me the house because I saw the ghost?"

"Now I've heard everything," Griff muttered.

Harry didn't hear him. "Anyway, getting back to the gardens, she insisted that she knew exactly how they should be laid out, and that's how it all began."

"Is that why they had to look like Versailles, because you were building them for the king of France?" she asked.

"That's exactly why. How could I question her when I felt the rightness of the idea from the very first minute I stuck a shovel in the earth? There was magic in the very air. It surrounded me. With every shrub I planted and every flower bed I laid out, I could feel it like a living presence. Everything I did was inspired. Everything I touched turned the place into a wonderland."

Nickie didn't know what to say. She'd experienced her own brand of magic at Bellefleur from the moment she'd set eyes on it as a child. But she didn't want to upset Griff, who seemed to be keeping himself on such an even keel in the face of all this otherworldly dialogue. His eyes were bright with repressed emotion but oddly enough, he didn't appear impatient or annoyed.

"That garden is enchanted," Harry insisted, glancing at each of them in turn. "Look what happened the minute you started to restore it, Griff—poof, he shows up again." He grinned disarmingly. "He appreciates your efforts, boy."

"But not enough to show himself to me."

Griff's reply threw Harry for a moment, but he bounced back quickly. "That's perfectly understandable," he said with a cheerful shrug. "He never appeared to me, either."

"I suppose we're not blue-blooded enough for his liking. After all, we're just lowly gardeners, and this guy was once a king."

"Why do you always have to impute the worst possible motives to him!" Nickie burst out. "There could be other reasons why he can't show himself to you. Maybe he's only allowed to appear to the owner of Bellefleur and related family members."

"I didn't realize ghosts had so many rules to follow," Griff said flippantly.

"It could be that he doesn't like your attitude," she pointed out with exaggerated patience.

"That makes us even, because I don't care for his, either. He thinks a woman should fall down at his feet just because he can pull off a soulful expression and knows how to bow."

Nickie couldn't help grinning as she rolled her eyes at him. "For someone who doesn't believe in the ghost you're pretty good at analyzing him."

"It's only for the sake of argument," he replied with a self-effacing grin. His eyes belied his casual assessment of the situation, for they held the faintest gleam of humor in their green depths, showing he realized very well that he'd gotten carried away. "It's all strictly hypothetical to me, but I just figured I'd play the role of devil's advocate for your benefit. And yours, Granddad."

She'd almost forgotten about Harry. She glanced over to find that he was sitting with his back against the pillows, his head cocked. He was obviously enjoying the lively sparring. When he caught her eye, he chuckled at her chagrined expression.

She couldn't resist one last retort. "That's very kind of you, Griff," she said. "It's a dirty job, but I suppose we should be grateful you're so willing to take it on."

Although they both questioned him further, Harry had nothing more to add to the basic facts he'd already revealed—that Marie-Claire believed the ghost was the king of France, that in spite of all his years at Bellefleur, Harry had never laid eyes on the apparition, although he swore he had felt his presence; and finally, that together owner and gardener had designed and built the gardens to resemble those at the great palace at Versailles so they would be fit for a king.

"We've got to be heading back, Granddad. Tell Tracy and Jack I'm sorry I missed them."

"Will do." Harry beamed.

"Is there anything you need before we leave?"

"No, thanks. I'm not helpless, you know. I'm supposed to get a lot of rest and take it easy, that's all.

Your visit has done me more good than a trainload of doctors peering down my throat and poking needles into me.''

Nickie had to agree the visit most certainly had. She said as much to Griff when they were on the road.

"Yeah," he said smugly. "I knew it would cheer him up to talk about that damned ghost, but I didn't expect those kind of results. Not that I'm complaining." He shook his head in amazement. "By the time we left, I swear he looked at least ten years younger."

"Those gardens mean a lot to him."

"They mean everything to him and always have. Once I finish sprucing up the place and you find a permanent gardener to maintain it, maybe he can come and see them every so often. That is, if you don't mind."

"Don't be ridiculous. He can come as often as he likes. He'll always be welcome at Bellefleur."

"Thank you."

She fiddled with the strap of her purse for a moment before getting up the nerve to ask the question uppermost on her mind. "So where do you stand on the question of the ghost now?" He didn't answer immediately, so she added, "Even if you still don't believe in him, I'll bet you can't help being intrigued by all this talk of kings."

There was another long pause, and then Griff answered in a careful voice, "You know, at first I was a hundred percent positive there was no ghost. I figured it was some strange phenomenon, one for the record books perhaps, but no ghost." He paused to glance over at her, his expression both rueful and enigmatic. "Now I don't know what to believe. I certainly can't explain what the hell is going on."

"That's a step in the right direction," she said lightly. "I've been thinking, though. I hate to throw a monkey wrench into an already complicated situation, but I just don't feel Charles was ever king of France. Maybe we're talking about different ghosts here."

"Good grief, isn't one enough?"

"It's either that, or my aunt was mistaken about his identity. No, listen," she said, holding up her hand to forestall whatever he was about to say. "Why would any French king come to America? And why would the king of France haunt a house in Tennessee?"

"Good question."

"Maybe my aunt just wanted him to be the king of France so badly that she fooled herself into believing he was. I'll be the first one to admit that Charles looks aristocratic, and he's certainly elegant, but he doesn't act like a king, especially not a French one."

"What do you mean?"

"From what I remember of my history, most members of the French royalty were horribly condescending to anyone who didn't belong to their class. Look at Marie Antoinette. She might have said, 'Let them eat cake,' out of ignorance at the conditions of the poor, but it still summed up the attitude of the upper classes. That's why the French Revolution, when it came, was so bloody and violent."

"Maybe your ghost is trying to break it to you gently by going incognito at first. Until he thinks you can handle the shock."

She made a noise of exasperation in her throat. "Will you get serious about this for once!"

He grinned, his white teeth flashing for a brief moment in the light of the street lamp they'd just driven under. "All right, take it easy." He checked the side mirror a second time before pulling out into the passing lane to get around a battered old truck piled with rickety furniture. "How about this. Perhaps he's not a king himself, but only connected with one in some fashion."

"You mean like a court painter? I suppose it's possible. It's certainly more likely that a court painter would end up coming to the United States. He might have been an aristocrat forced to flee the guillotine." She worried her lip. "We still need more to go on. All this is just speculation."

By now they'd left the congestion of Memphis far behind. Traffic on the highway was light. There was nothing to see but farmland and the occasional billboard advertising food and lodging. Nickie stirred restlessly in her seat as her mind worked on the problem.

"How about his clothes?" Griff asked. "You could find out when they were wearing similar apparel."

"True. And I suppose we shouldn't dismiss this king business out of hand, either. I know Louis *XIV* built Versailles, so I assume he was the one responsible for the gardens, too. And Louis *XVI* was the one they guillotined during the French Revolution. It doesn't give us a large time frame to work with, because France didn't have a king again until Louis XVIII, and according to my aunt his reign only lasted ten years before he died."

"What happened to King Louis XVII?"

"There wasn't one. He was still a child when he died, sometime during the Revolution. That's how my alleged ancestral relative, the Comte de Provence got to become Louis XVIII—he waited around until the dust had settled after Napoleon's rule."

"You're descended from a French king?"

She shook her head, smiling as she recalled her aunt's vehement pride on the subject. "Not exactly. According to my aunt, we're related to the same branch of the family, but of course our side emigrated here and his side stayed there."

"Maybe that's the king your aunt was referring to."

"The thought did cross my mind, but I'm afraid it's out of the question." At his frown she went on to explain, "There's a copy of a painting of him hanging in the dining room. Even in all his royal glory, he was not a handsome man." One corner of her mouth tilted up crookedly as she visualized the portrait in question. "I realize he was past his prime when it was painted, but I'm positive he never looked like Charles in his youth, not in a million years."

"I'm beginning to think no one can measure up to your paragon of a ghost. No wonder I find it hard to believe in him—he's too damn perfect."

Nickie raised her eyebrows but declined to comment. It would only land her in trouble. Griff didn't have anything to worry about in any comparison with the ghost. Sure, both were handsome; both had extraordinary eyes and a noticeable presence. But Griff was flesh and blood and infinitely preferable in her eyes. He was more rugged than Charles, muscular where Charles was slim. Imagining him in period dress nearly took her breath away. The fitted pants would cling lovingly to his long legs, and those ruffles at the throat and wrists would play against Griff's green eyes and strong hands. The image made her pulse quicken, especially when she put herself into the picture clad in a low-cut gown with voluminous skirts, petticoats and undergarments Griff would have no trouble removing. His strong fingers would dispose of such obstacles with determination and skill, the way he handled everything else.

She could feel the heat flooding her cheeks. Thank goodness they were making the turn onto Main Street, which meant they were almost home. She definitely needed something to interrupt her wayward thoughts. She forced her attention to the view of the stone walls and gate house that signaled the approach to Bellefleur.

Griff dropped her off at the front stairs, then pulled the car a short distance away to park it. Nickie climbed the steps in a dreamlike trance, all the things she'd learned about the ghost from Griff's grandfather whirling around in her head, along with the speculations she hadn't voiced aloud. She'd never really doubted the ghost's presence in her life, but what she'd learned today helped to reinforce it, although the sense of unreality discussing him always brought couldn't be entirely dissipated.

As she turned the key in the lock, she realized she was hearing music. The sound of Griff's slamming the car door faded into the background in the face of the beautiful lilting melody that twined around her senses and filled her head. It sounded like a flute, or possibly a recorder. In any case, it possessed a timeless quality that sounded right at home in Bellefleur. She paused in the doorway, her head cocked to one side as she tried to better pull in the sound.

Where could it be coming from? she wondered dreamily. None of Bellefleur's neighbors were situated very close, but perhaps the still night air was acting as a conduit. As she slowly removed her key and pushed open the door, the notes grew louder, rising in a breathtaking crescendo, fluttering there for a timeless moment and then descending down the musical scale to pick up the main melody once again.

With a start she realized the music was coming from inside the house.

# *Chapter Eight*

Nickie's throat tightened momentarily in a combination of fascination and alarm as she stood there, one hand on the screen door, the other clutching the lintel as she listened spellbound to the enchanting melody. It was a sprightly little ditty, airy and joyful, something she could imagine being played for the sheer solitary enjoyment of its perpetrator.

The last note was just dying away when she heard Griff's foot hit the bottom stair. He must have realized that something was going on, because he quickly sprinted up the remaining stairs. She turned to face him, letting the screen door scrape shut behind her and leaning her now limp body against the cool shingles of the house. She knew her face bore a bemused expression of wonderment.

"Not again," Griff muttered.

He sounded annoyed. He *was* annoyed, she realized, noticing his hands clenched into fists at his sides. Before she knew what was happening, he had reached out to grab her shoulders, hauling her against his hard body and lowering his head to fuse his mouth with hers. His emotions were suddenly running high, and the kiss was hard and demanding. It was quite a jarring contrast after the liquid notes that still echoed in her head, but she made the transition easily as the urgency of his lips called forth an answering response from deep inside her.

Finding it difficult to stand upright under her own power, she relaxed further against the wall of the house. His body immediately followed hers, surrounding her and warming her with incredible heat as he slanted his mouth first one way, then the other, as if to devour her. He didn't give her time to think; he simply took her breath away.

As suddenly as it had begun it ended. He stepped back, leaving Nickie dazed.

"What was that for?" she asked, automatically bringing the back of her hand up to touch her throbbing lips. Her confusion at his abrupt retreat was stamped all over her face, along with her acute disappointment.

"I'm glad to see that something besides that stupid spook can cause that expression in your eyes."

"He's not a stupid spook," she replied distractedly, more for something to say than because she was upset at his statement. She was feeling too soft and pliable to argue with him, especially when she was beginning to suspect he was jealous of her ghost.

He reached for her hands and squeezed them soothingly before using them to leverage her back into his embrace. "I'm sorry. I didn't mean to be so rough."

"You weren't," she denied against his shirt. If that was rough, she shivered at the thought of his gentleness.

It felt so good to be held in his arms. His chest was a solid bulwark against her resolution to keep this man at a safe distance. She didn't even let the thought materialize. It was just a vague niggle in the back of her mind, and she left it there. Everything else had already fled from her conscious thoughts, including the music.

She rubbed her cheek dreamily against his shirt. She could feel the hard muscle underneath. The potent masculine scent of his body, a combination of clothes and skin and after-shave, melted her resistance away. She raised her face to look at him, hoping he would kiss her again.

But he was gazing down at her with steely eyes, as if bracing himself for unpleasant news. She had so lost her bearings she hadn't the faintest idea why that should be until he spoke. "What happened this time?"

She sighed. She knew her answer was about to wipe out her last hope for more intimacy. "I heard music," she replied softly, dropping her arms from around his lean waist before he could withdraw first. Even to her own ears the explanation sounded lame after the sharply physical reality of their heated kiss. "It was coming from inside the house."

"Music?" He frowned. This was obviously not what he'd expected to hear. "You mean you didn't see the ghost again?"

"No."

"You just heard music?"

She nodded. "Yes."

"What kind of music? Can you hear it now?"

"No, it's gone." She dared a glance at his stony features, then quickly looked away. "It sounded like a flute." How could he be so distant? Why didn't he want to kiss her when only moments ago he'd seemed so desperate for her mouth?

He made a nondescript noise as he pulled open the screen door and gestured her inside. "It was probably a radio. Come on, let's go check it out."

She didn't bother to argue, although she was sure it hadn't been a radio. She knew she had a good imagination, but she also knew she could never have conjured up the way those notes floated through the air, landing caressingly on her eardrums like the voice of a soulful lover. It had been too present, too real, the melody much too rounded and full to have come from the speakers of a radio, even if it was possible.

Instead of following Griff into the sitting room, she found herself automatically heading for the music room. Where else but there to begin a search for the origins of the mysterious melody? Holding her breath, she groped along the wall to find the switch and flicked on the lights. Even though she knew what to expect, the beauty of the room still washed over her like the grand finale of the lushest symphony, stopping the breath in her throat.

An imposing grand piano held the place of honor, just slightly off center in the middle of the room, its bench neatly pushed beneath the keyboard. The lid was closed and its polished surface gleamed under the artificial lighting like the finest ebony. Nearby, a gold harp sat like a beautiful swan, a small stool tucked next to it. She remembered her aunt telling her it had been designed by John Fortesquieu back in 1790. A sewing necessaire, shaped like a globe and with signs of the zodiac inlaid in exotic woods, indicated that the room could be used for more utilitarian purposes, as well as for nourishing the soul.

Across the room from the large arched windows, the wall was completely covered with mirrors, divided by five red marble pilasters with gilt bases. A marble niche in the center boasted a statue of a violinist in a frock coat, done in marble and porphyry. The piano had been placed so that the player could see himself reflected in flattering golden hues.

Nickie walked into the center of the room, gazing around with pride and awe, things she always felt when confronted with the beauty of Bellefleur. She could just imagine how this room must have looked during an impromptu recital, bathed in flickering candlelight. A golden fairyland couldn't be more beautiful.

She heard Griff behind her. "Did you find anything?" she asked.

"No. I checked, but the TV wasn't on. And I couldn't find the radio."

She smiled. "That's because there isn't one. I have a small portable in a box upstairs in my room, but I haven't unpacked it yet. It almost seems a sacrilege to play modern music in a place like this."

"Yeah, well, you could have told me."

She grinned. "I didn't want to spoil your fun."

"Thanks."

Ignoring his droll tone, she wandered idly around the room. She didn't know what she was looking for, but she couldn't seem to turn around and walk out. As she circled the piano she noticed that there was something lying behind the scroll-like wood frame used to hold sheets of music. She moved closer.

"Griff, look at this."

There was a strange-looking instrument lying along the edge of the piano, just above the closed keyboard. She carefully picked it up and held it out for his inspection.

"Oh no, you're not thinking..." His voice trailed off as his gaze raked her face. His worst fears were confirmed as he read the conclusion in her eyes. "Don't tell me he can play a musical instrument, along with everything else," he scoffed, sarcasm apparent in his voice. "Is there no end to his talents?"

He took the peculiar instrument from her hand. It had four finger holes on the top and two thumbholes on the bottom and a thinner section that tapered gracefully into the mouthpiece.

"What is this thing, anyway?" he asked.

"I don't know. Some kind of flute?"

"Don't you play a flute holding it to the side?" He held the instrument in front of his mouth, simulating the way it should be played. "This thing looks like you tackle it straight on. I also thought flutes had a larger diameter."

"Maybe it's a recorder or something. We'll have to look it up."

Griff had barely handed it back to her when they were startled by a sharp noise from above. It sounded like something had crashed to the floor in one of the rooms upstairs. Nickie gripped the cylindrical body of the instrument in both hands as she stared upward. Of course, there was nothing to see but the ceiling.

"What now?" Griff demanded in a testy voice. He obviously didn't expect an answer, because he was already sprinting out the door.

Nickie hurried to join him. By the time she reached the second floor, Griff was coming out of the Blue Salon.

"What about the library?" Nickie asked breathlessly.

"I was just about to check it."

He switched on the light and stepped over the threshold. She followed him into its leather-scented interior, breathing deeply.

"That's your culprit," he said, pointing.

She saw a book lying facedown on the floor, some of its pages crumpled. Gazing up, she saw the open slot in the center of the shelf one from the top. The book must have fallen from there. The ladder, which could be rolled along the entire wall was located exactly next to the spot. She watched Griff lean down, his hands surprisingly gentle as he plucked the volume from the floor. He smoothed the bent pages respectfully before turning it over to look at the title. He didn't speak for several long moments, and then he held it up so she could read it for herself.

It took her a moment to decipher the single word embossed on the front cover, so elaborate was the lettering. *"Register,"* she finally breathed in wonder.

He held it out to her. "Here," he said. "Why don't you see what's inside."

"Okay."

She accepted the volume with a grateful nod, feeling its hefty weight before she opened it to the front page. The ink was so faded it had turned from black to brown, but she could still make out the bold script on the title page. "'Bellefleur, 1817,'" she read aloud, her voice quickening with excitement. "That's only a couple of years after this place was built."

"Who actually built Bellefleur?"

"A Frenchman named Jean-Paul Clermont. My great-aunt told me that wasn't his real name, that he was a nobleman with a title, but he dropped it after arriving here."

She could feel Griff watching her as she thumbed quickly through the book, her gaze narrowed in concentration as her mind computed what was on the pages.

"It seems to be some kind of housekeeping record. Look, here's a dinner menu for an 'oyster party,' whatever that is. And here's a list of the guests attending a musical soiree given on 15 September." She ran her finger down the page as she began reading them off. "Mr. and Mrs. Wilson Proffer, Miss Georgina Hauser, Monsieur Gervaise Guillaume de la Forêt." She raised shining eyes to his. "This is perfect. We're bound to find some kind of clue to Charles's identity."

Griff's expression softened at her enthusiasm. "Or discover if the king of France ever dined here. Or any other king, for that matter."

Her smile widened. "Exactly." She flipped through the pages again. "It isn't very long—a lot of it appears to be lists and recipes. I can probably get through it tonight."

"Be my guest."

"But first I want to check something else." She walked to the bottom shelf where the books were bound in buckram, indicating their more modern origins. "I know I saw a title on music somewhere... Ah, here it is."

She pulled out a slim volume that still retained its paper dustcover although the edges were curling and frayed. She flipped it open. "Here we go—the flute family."

Griff peered over her shoulder as they studied the page of drawings. "There it is," he said, pointing.

"Flageolet," she said, reading the caption underneath before turning puzzled eyes to Griff. "Flageolet? I've never heard of it."

"Let me see that." He took the book from her unresisting hands. "'A small, end-blown flute of the recorder family that has four finger holes in front and two in the rear.'"

"'Common in Europe during the seventeenth and eighteenth centuries, especially in France,'" she continued reading when he stopped. "'Its popularity died out during the nineteenth century.'"

She clasped her hands tightly as a hot burst of energy and excitement licked up her spine. "Griff, this fits right in with what we know about Charles. If he did come to Bellefleur, it could have been during those early years, when the Clermonts lived here. They were French émigrés, and we're assuming Charles was also French. Maybe they knew each other in France before the revolution." Her eyes widened as she whispered tautly, "Maybe they were all part of Louis XVI's court!"

"It makes sense," Griff agreed thoughtfully. "Although this guy is so talented we don't know if he was the court painter or the court musician."

Nickie smiled to herself. Griff was talking as if Charles was an acquaintance. She'd known he couldn't resist a puzzle, no matter how farfetched the parameters. Perhaps he was even starting to believe in the ghost of Bellefleur. "He could have been just a regular garden-variety nobleman," she pointed out. "Along with the rest of their studies, they were often taught to play an instrument, sketch and dance. Although I can't imagine everyone being as talented as Charles."

"There you go again," he muttered.

She chuckled. "I can't help it if he's a multitalented, eighteenth-century kind of guy. I'm sure if you'd had the tutors his father probably hired, you'd turn out just like him."

"Somehow I doubt it."

"That's all right. You have other qualities."

"Do I?" he whispered. She'd been teasing, but suddenly the atmosphere had shifted to something dangerously sensuous.

He laid the book aside and took her by the shoulders, turning her around until she faced him. "Like what?"

She licked her lips and swallowed hard, even though she knew it was a dead giveaway of her reaction to his nearness. He must have already known how he affected her. "Like your ability in mathematics."

"What else? There must be something more pleasing to a woman's heart than that. Look at your ghost. He's tall and handsome. He charms you with elegant manners, beautiful music, wonderful drawings. What can I possibly do to compete?"

He grasped her just above the wrists, lifting her arms and placing them around his neck. When they started sliding limply down his chest, he did it again. This time she got the message and left them hooked behind his head. Then he wrapped his arms around her waist, tugging her closer as he waited for her answer.

No wonder he'd been so accommodating about the ghost just a few moments ago. He'd merely been biding his time, humoring her until he could spring this sensual assault on her. She knew she should resist, but at the moment she didn't care about practical sensible behavior. Having a ghost in your life tended to make reckless behavior seem ordinary, and ordinary behavior dull. Yes indeed, seeing Charles had caused more than one aspect of her life to appear as colorless as an old black-and-white movie.

But Griff came across in definite, full-blown technicolor.

He leaned closer, his mouth moving slowly from her cheek toward her ear, placing kisses along the way. When he finally arrived at his destination, he said in a husky voice, "I figure I have one immediate advantage over him—I'm the guy who's here with you now, because I'm the guy who's made of flesh and blood." He nibbled on her earlobe, and she couldn't suppress the shiver of excitement that flickered up her spine. "Just like you."

She closed her eyes. "I never denied it."

"That's a step in the right direction," he said softly, echoing her earlier words. His hands moved toward her shoulders, making enticing patterns on her back through the material of her blouse. "We could make it a natural progression and take the next step."

"I don't think that's very wise."

"Is everything you do wise?"

She sighed. "Of course not. But there are some things that experience has tried to teach me, and I'd be foolish not to listen and learn."

"Like what?" he murmured.

She could tell he thought she was only offering him the standard tried-and-true feminine excuse, but that wasn't the case. She gazed up at him sadly. "My father's a salesman. When I was growing up we moved from one place to another like a band of Gypsies. We never stayed more than two or three years in any one location." She shook her head as the painful memories flooded back. "I've been forced to say goodbye more times than I can count. I finally figured out that it was easier not to get involved in the first place, not when you knew you were only going to be moving away."

"Yeah, but now you're all grown-up. You're the one who calls the shots, not your parents."

"That's true. And that's what I intend to do. But don't you see how diametrically opposed our thinking on this subject is? I've finally managed to put down roots. You're more like a migrating bird, making a brief stopover before moving on. I've had enough migrating to last me a lifetime."

He dropped his hands to his sides. "Aren't we being poetic this evening," he said in a rough strained voice that matched the tension around his eyes. "I can speak in metaphors, too. You may have decided to put down roots, but that still doesn't make you a damn tree.''

His gaze burned into her like green fire. She closed her eyes against it and swallowed hard, hoping to keep the tears from clogging her throat. She just couldn't get involved with someone who wanted that kind of life-style, not when she knew so well how miserable it was to be rootless, to be part of a community on the surface and yet never really belonging because you wouldn't be staying.

Well, now she did have a place to belong to, a place that needed her. She felt safe and secure at Bellefleur, something she realized she'd never really felt as a child. Some people might say she'd clipped her own wings, but she didn't see it that way.

She opened her eyes to find Griff watching her, his gaze hooded, his expression unreadable. All this was his fault, anyway, she thought, trying to muster up some self-righteous indignation but failing miserably. She'd been ecstatic living at Bellefleur until he'd come along with his sexy green eyes and dark brooding looks.

''No,'' she whispered.

He took her at her word. ''Fine,'' he said, stepping farther away from her. ''Since you insist on predicting the outcome of this relationship before it's even begun, I'll leave you to it.''

He strode to the door, but stopped just before he reached the threshold, his body stiff and tense as he turned to face her. ''I hate to disillusion you, but did you ever stop to think that maybe I'm just as likely to crash and burn over this thing as you are? At least I'm not trying to second-guess what the final outcome will be." His jaw muscles clenched visibly in the dim light. "At least I'm not so cut off from life that I'm unwilling to take a chance on it."

She longed to defend herself from his hurtful accusations. She even opened her mouth to speak, but the words of protest she tried to formulate died on her lips for lack of substance. What could she say when he was basically correct, even if the terms in which he couched it made her appear a coward. She had simply taught herself to be practical, nothing more. Griff couldn't seem to come to terms with that.

He noted her inner struggles without sympathy, a cynical smile on his face. "Don't worry, Nickie. I'll be out of your hair in a couple more days. I'm sure you'll be very happy with only your ghost for company, since the two of you have so much in common."

"What do you mean?" she couldn't stop herself from asking.

He ticked the reasons off on his fingers. "You're artists, you both live at Bellefleur, which in itself is like an impossible dream, and you're both harder to grasp than a will-o'-the-wisp. Sweet dreams, Mademoiselle DuPrés," he added, tossing the words over his shoulder with cool carelessness as he stalked out the door. "Sweet, insubstantial dreams."

## Chapter Nine

By the time the next day dawned, Griff found himself longing to jump into his car and tear out of Belle-fleur's courtyard. He could almost hear the spitting sound of flying gravel beneath his wheels as he peeled onto the street. But the thought of his grandfather sobered him. He recalled the enormous change that had come over the old man upon hearing that the damned ghost was back. Griff could almost swear he'd witnessed an instant recovery. With that in mind, he forced himself to march straight out to the toolshed.

After all, what he'd said to Nickie last night was true. A couple more days of intensive labor would see the gardens looking respectable, although he couldn't say they would be as immaculate as when his grandfather had cared for them. Nevertheless, he knew his grandfather would be pleased with the results. He only hoped the old man would think the damned spook was also satisfied.

Even after a full day of intensive labor to clear his head, Griff was still in no mood for conversation later that evening when he returned to the house. He didn't hear any sounds, so he figured Nickie must be working in her study.

He tiptoed quietly up the stairs and slipped into the bathroom before she could discover he was back. If nothing else, he needed a shower, not only to wash the dirt from his body but to help clear his clogged brain. Nothing else today had been able to bring him back to the realm of normality. He realized he hadn't experienced an entire normal day since he'd walked up Bellefleur's driveway.

He adjusted the water, then stepped into the large bathing area with a rueful grin. He couldn't even take a simple shower without being surrounded by gilt and luxury. What was wrong with a simple stall fitted out with a stainless-steel shower head and faucets?

The only normal predictable occurrence was his desire for Nickie. That emotion seemed to burn like a laser beam of truth through all the other foolishness that surrounded him and Bellefleur. He wanted her and she wanted him, but she'd convinced herself she knew the outcome of their attraction and had flung it up as a barrier. What could he say to counter something that hadn't even happened yet? He didn't stand a chance.

Hunger drove him downstairs after his shower. There was still no sign of Nickie, so he foraged in the refrigerator, one of the few things in this place that wasn't decked out in fancy wallpaper or gilt. A noise alerted him, and he turned just in time to see Nickie waltz into the kitchen. The description was no exaggeration.

"I made an important discovery this afternoon!" she declared.

Her face glowed as she halted in the middle of the floor. Griff could see she was having trouble restraining herself. Well, so was he. Her excitement was contagious, even though he knew it originated from a different source than the pure physical awareness that was heating his blood. He wanted to take her in his arms and pick up where they'd left off last night.

"I know who the ghost is," she said, smiling broadly.

To hell with the ghost, he thought as he stared at her. He knew his hunger must be reflected in his eyes, but Nickie was too enthralled with her impending announcement to notice. If she thought the revelation of the ghost's identity would cause him to forget certain highlights of their encounter last night, she was seriously mistaken.

"I know who he is," she repeated in a cheerfully coaxing voice. "And he's not the king of France."

"Who?" In spite of his hard-nosed attitude about the ghost until now, he had to admit he was curious.

"John James Audubon."

"John James . . . Audubon?" He was shocked and he knew his face showed it. His brow wrinkled as he shifted gears to take in this latest development. "You mean the guy who ran around America painting pictures of birds?"

He didn't think it was possible, but her grin widened. "That's the one."

"How do you know?"

"Follow me and I'll show you."

He could think of other places he'd rather follow her to, but he let her lead him from the room.

"That register we found was a godsend," she said as she trotted up the stairs by his side. She suddenly chuckled. "Or maybe that should be ghostsend."

He shot her a droll look but didn't rise to the bait.

"I wrote down all the names I found anywhere on its pages. And then I tried to find portraits of them," she explained, the words tumbling out of her mouth in excitement. "I figured the more obscure people would be harder to find, if I could find them at all, so I left them until last. Instead, I went for the names I recognized, figuring I could eliminate them right off the bat before getting down to the real hunt."

They reached the landing. Thank goodness this time there were no flowers on the Louis XIV table. Nickie bounced up the rest of the stairs, beckoning him to hurry.

"I never dreamed we were housing such a famous ghost," she continued, leading him into the study. "But there he was, smiling at me from the frontispiece of *Birds of America,* a book that was right here at Bellefleur! Wasn't that incredibly lucky?"

"Incredibly," he murmured, coming to a halt just inside the door.

She crossed to her desk and picked up a large thick volume. After carrying it over to Griff, she flipped to the frontispiece and held it so he could see, supporting the heavy weight of the book along one arm and against her collarbone. "Well," she announced dramatically, "there he is!"

Griff's stomach muscles clenched. "That's what he looks like?"

"That's him."

"That's exactly like him?"

"Yes, of course. That's what I'm trying to tell you." She bit her lip thoughtfully as she peered over the top, studying the portrait upside down. "This is definitely a very good likeness."

Holy smokes, he thought in dismay as he snatched the book from her. His fingers gripped the binding as he gazed at the portrait with unwilling fascination. He was no real judge of what a woman might like in a male, but he had the sinking feeling that this guy qualified big time. He was right up there in a class with Rhett Butler and Robin Hood, a romantic vision of manhood of days gone by. His luminous eyes gazed at Griff guilelessly from the page.

"Well, say something," she demanded.

"I'm surprised you didn't tell me to stick to gardening and bridge building."

"He is an eyeful, isn't he?" she agreed teasingly. "But that's not what I meant. I want to know what you think about the ghost being Audubon."

"What's he got to do with the French aristocracy?" He asked the first question that popped into his head. Most of his brain power was still focused on the handsome artist. "I thought he was American."

"He was." She reached over to scoop up another volume from the desktop, this one smaller but almost as thick. "See, it says right here, 'U.S. naturalist who painted birds.'"

He gazed where her finger pointed and nodded. "So he's a local fellow."

"Not exactly. Listen to this: 'No one knows where Audubon came from originally. He was adopted at a young age by Jean Audubon, a Frenchman, in Les Cayes, Haiti.' So he still has some French connections, although not the kind we thought. Not that it matters," she added with a shrug, setting down the book. "The bottom line is that he's not a king or an aristocrat or anyone else connected with Louis XVI's court. According to this he was born in 1785 so he was a mere child of nine when Louis and Marie Antoinette were beheaded."

"You sound disappointed," he said with a smile. He was beginning to calm down from the initial shock of learning about the ghost's likeness to Audubon. "Isn't a famous naturalist enough for you?"

"I'm not disappointed. Well, only a little," she admitted. "It would have been exciting to know it was a king roaming the corridors. And you have to admit that Bellefleur provides the perfect setting for one."

"True."

"I also checked to see if there were any mislaid royal descendants, just to cover all the possibilities. Louis XVI had a son, the young dauphin, who technically became Louis XVII after his parents' execution. But he died while he was being held prisoner in Paris."

"I see," Griff murmured since some sort of response seemed required.

"So, I guess my aunt did get carried away, just as we suspected all along." Nickie laughed, shaking her head.

"I think we've all gotten a little carried away...."

"Maybe that's what he was trying to tell us all along—that he wasn't a king, just an artist and naturalist. After all, he was carrying around that sketchbook. He was probably tired of being an impostor and was trying to set the record straight."

Griff nodded. It made sense in the same crazy kind of way everything about this place made sense.

"That would also explain why he wanted so much to go outside. Hey, I just thought of something else." She pressed her palms together as though she was praying, tapping her two index fingers against her chin. "He's probably responsible for that gang of birds that hangs around here all the time. They come to pay him homage for having painted such beautiful pictures of them."

Griff slanted her an amused skeptical glance from beneath his brows.

"Then how do *you* explain that raucous mob outside the second-floor windows?" she asked.

"An abundance of insects. A perfect resting place before flying down to enter the garden."

She waved his explanation aside. "All right, never mind the birds." She gazed toward the window wistfully. "Do you think this means he won't be back now that we've discovered his secret?"

*I hope I'm that lucky,* Griff thought. "It sounds perfectly logical to me."

"Yeah, and I bet I know why." She waggled her finger at him, but he only smiled serenely. "You won't have to deal with him anymore."

He tried to inject regret into his expression, but he couldn't stop his smile from broadening. "Just when I was starting to get the hang of this apparition business."

It looked like the ghost hunt was over. At least Nickie seemed satisfied that it was. He realized he felt a sharp pang of regret at the thought of returning to the rational world. He had to admit he'd enjoyed getting caught up in Bellefleur's tide of magic, moonlight and madness.

He glanced at Nickie's lovely profile, and his insides tightened with the same gut-level reaction her delicate ivory-hued features always aroused in him. In his opinion she was the perfect female, slim and leggy, just the right size and shape to fill a man's arms. He remembered how melting and luminous her brown eyes had become after he'd kissed her. He could almost feel her soft, eager mouth pressing against his, and he ached.

She was busy thumbing through another book, so he took the opportunity to continue to stare at her. Of course if he was still temporarily bewitched, he couldn't be held responsible for his actions. He wondered what she would do if he kissed her again. He saw no reason she should continue fighting the tide when *he* had finally given it up. If Bellefleur was magic, then they were meant to come together here. As he'd said to her before, the ghost might be handsome and accomplished, but he was the one who was here in the flesh, and only he could give her physical satisfaction to go along with the emotion.

He found he wanted to, badly. She couldn't refuse, not when he needed her so much. He wanted to absorb her very essence into his body and soul. He was not the kind of man to accept defeat as a foregone conclusion. She might be able to coolly decide that their romance was doomed, that distance would eventually sever any ties they might forge, but he suddenly found he couldn't live another minute without at least trying to make her understand his side of things.

"Nickie," he said softly.

Her head shot up like a wary gazelle's, graceful but acutely alert as if she sensed danger. "What?"

He walked over to her and gently pried the book from her fingers. She resisted, but only for a moment before shrugging congenially and letting him take it. He reached over to set it on the desk before turning back to her.

"I'm not buying it anymore."

"Buying what?" She frowned. "Do you mean about handling the ghost? Well, that was short-lived."

He slipped his arms around her waist and pulled her close. Her eyes widened in faint distress, but she didn't pull away. It was almost as if she thought a sudden movement might set him off. She probably wasn't far wrong.

"I'm not talking about the ghost," he explained patiently. He moved his hands in a caressing motion up her arms and across her shoulders until he was gently cupping her face. "I'm talking about the reason you gave me for avoiding this." He bent forward and kissed her lightly on the lips.

"I didn't ask you to buy it, only to honor it."

"I don't even think you want to honor it. Not if you're totally honest with yourself."

A shadow flickered in the depths of her brown eyes. "What do you expect me to do?" she asked in exasperation.

He kissed her again. "Take a chance, just as I'm prepared to do. Grab life with both hands." He caressed the smooth skin along her cheekbones with his thumbs. "Anyone who stays in a house with a ghost certainly isn't lacking in courage."

"As I recall, I didn't have much of a choice about that," she said with a crooked grin, continuing to avoid his direct gaze. "He seems to live here."

"Aaah, I see. That gives him a certain hold over you."

"I suppose that's true." She ducked her head. "But he doesn't have the power to hurt me the way you do."

Griff felt a fierce joy surge through his body at her admission. "Lady, it's not a one-way street, you know. You can hurt me just as deeply."

Now she did look into his eyes, searching their depths to gauge his sincerity. "Can I?" she asked gently. "Or would it just be wounded male pride?"

"Damn you, Nickie, it involves a hell of a lot more than wounded male pride." He held her face immobile. He didn't want her to be able to avoid seeing the passionate conviction he knew blazed in his eyes. He could feel the heat from it himself. His entire body burned. "Actually, it takes a bloody fool to even try to compete with a famous naturalist and a house fit for a king."

"Is that what you think this is all about?"

"Isn't it?" he growled.

"You're right, you are a fool," she told him. But there was no sting in the harsh words—they were whispered like a tender endearment and her eyes glowed with warm invitation. He felt the repercussions from her abrupt about-face zap from the top of his head to the soles of his feet like an electric current.

He lowered his mouth toward hers once more, then halted only inches away. "If you want me to stop, now would be a good time to say so," he informed her in a low voice.

He didn't know where his chivalrous restraint was coming from or how much longer it was going to last, but he realized with a deep aching certainty that he didn't care if Nickie tumbled into his arms and his bed by default. He figured once she was there, he'd be able to convince her to stay, if only through the overwhelming force of his longing.

Her arms tensed against his neck. "I can't do it," she groaned, closing her eyes against his probing stare.

Pain stabbed through his gut and tightened his throat, but he forced himself to speak. "Can't do what? Can't let me make love to you?"

She opened her eyes and met his gaze unflinchingly. "I can't say the words to stop you."

He couldn't help grinning with pleasure at this admission. Nickie certainly didn't shy away from telling the truth, no matter how uncomfortable it might make her feel. She always met things head-on. It was one of the things he admired about her. "But you wish you could, don't you?"

"Of course I wish I could. This whole thing is suicidal." She reached up to touch his face, her expression tender. "But right now I just don't seem to care."

"That makes two of us."

He closed the rest of the distance to cover her mouth with his, this time allowing no mental fetters to get in his way. The freedom of it poured through his body like liquid fire. It was a delicious sensation and a powerful one, that went to his head like Bellefleur's finest brandy, especially when he realized that Nickie was returning his kisses as eagerly as he was giving them.

He slipped one hand between their bodies and covered her breast. His palm burned where it touched her body, and he could feel her nipple tighten right through the layers of her clothes. He groaned and pushed his hand inside her blouse and bra until he could caress her soft skin. The sensation of her nipple against his palm ignited an explosion of heat within him just beneath the surface of his skin. He could feel the perspiration sliding down his brow as he caressed and molded her flesh. He couldn't seem to slow down. He was on fire.

The hell with the finer nuances, he thought as he kissed her throat. They'd been analyzing their attraction to death to no good purpose. It was inevitable that they come together. Hadn't he known it from the start?

He was damned if he was going to let this opportunity to bond with Nickie slip away. He wasn't an impulsive man, but he found himself riding his impulses now. Logic had nothing to do with this. He wanted her and she wanted him. Wasn't it worth the risk to try to forge these ties with her? To have something he could build on? He wasn't sure the opportunity would arise again.

"I swore I wouldn't do this," she murmured breathlessly, clinging to his shoulders as he left her mouth to press heated kisses along her throat. "I guess I don't have much willpower."

He usually felt uncomfortable verbalizing his innermost emotions, especially when they involved flowery compliments to a woman. But he suddenly found himself responding from the depths of his heart. "You don't need willpower when you're brave and beautiful and can handle anything and anyone."

"Even you?"

"Especially me."

He reached down and scooped her up into his arms. When she didn't protest, he headed for her bedroom, hoping against hope that she was as beyond rational thought as he was. In spite of his earlier promise to himself, he dreaded having her come to her senses just in time to tell him once again how she shouldn't be doing these things with him. As far as he was concerned it was too late to turn back, and he was afraid that if she tried to stop him now, he would shatter into a thousand pieces.

But she only wrapped her arms around his neck, kissing his throat as he carried her along the hallway. He elbowed his way past the door and carried her to the huge four-poster that dominated the room. He didn't have to lower her to place her on it, because the top of the mattress came to his waist. He merely released her onto the covers and used the small stool that stood beside the bed to vault up after her.

"Griff?"

He froze. "What?"

She scooted closer, reaching for his hand and bringing it to her face so she could rub her cheek against it. His heart started beating again. "I wonder how long it's been since anyone made love at Bellefleur."

He caressed her face for a moment before freeing his captured hand, using it instead to unbutton her blouse. "Obviously, way too long." He hardly knew what he was saying, so intense was his concentration on the task at hand.

"I swear this house is magic. Can you feel it?" She pushed herself up on one elbow, using her free hand to emphasize her point. "I did from the first moment I set eyes on this place."

"Forget about Bellefleur for once," he commanded in a low growl. "Forget about everything except the way I'm going to make you feel."

He heard her soft sigh as he finally pushed the material of her blouse apart. His hand caressed the smooth flesh of her stomach, moving inexorably upward until he was once again cupping her breast.

"I think I wanted to make love to you from the first moment I set eyes on you. And I can honestly say that Bellefleur had nothing to do with it."

She reached for the hem of his T-shirt, pulling it free from the waistband of his pants and pushing the material toward his shoulders. She ran her hands up his torso in a slow provocative motion, her eyes soft with longing as she smiled at him. He wanted to drown in that smile.

"How come we can never seem to agree about why things happen around here?"

He tried to grin, but it was more a baring of his teeth, because his face was taut with desire. "I don't know, but once we get past that initial conflict, everything seems to move along just fine."

He pulled the shirt over his head and tossed it aside. So what if they didn't agree on things. Nothing in this world was ever perfect, unless you counted the reverent look in Nickie's eyes as she gazed at his body. She reached out with both hands, stroking his chest and nearly sending him over the edge. He closed his eyes against the vivid flood of sensations that tightened his body and made him want to grab her and take her. He didn't want to go too fast. He wanted their time together to last as long as he could manage to hold on to his self-control.

And yet, instead of stopping her, he urged her to continue by placing his hands over hers in a silent gesture of approval and permission, guiding them lower on his body until he thought he would explode from the pleasure. He quickly moved them back up above his waist, holding them in place with one hand while he used the other to fumble with the opening of his pants. It seemed like forever before he finally succeeded in pulling them down over his hips. He then lowered himself to the bed, offering his body like a pagan sacrifice and knowing that a large chunk of his heart went along with it.

She accepted the offer, continuing to caress him without the slightest hesitation. Only now she'd added the touch of her mouth. Everywhere her lips pressed against his heated flesh, every place her teeth nibbled, burned with pleasure.

He gazed up at the dark material of the canopy over his head, feeling like a pasha in a Turkish harem. His body was experiencing so much pleasure he thought he would burst out of his skin; he had to force himself to lie still and let her have her way with him. He knew he wasn't going to be able to keep his cool much longer. He could think of nothing better in this life than to have her hands on him forever, but he ached to reciprocate.

"Yes, Nickie," he groaned, his head tossing restlessly on the pillow as her hand moved to caress and fondle the part of his body where all his urges were centered.

He wanted to tell her how much she was pleasing him, how beautiful she was and how everything she was doing to him was perfect beyond measure, but there were no words to describe what he was experiencing. He would have to tell her the way she was telling him, with his hands, his mouth and his body.

He quickly rolled over, taking Nickie with him and pressing her down into the mattress. He felt triumphant, as if he had won a fierce battle against overwhelming odds and conquered a kingdom. He couldn't wait another minute to finish undressing her.

"I want to be able to touch you everywhere," he whispered, pulling the blouse from her body and setting to work on her white jeans, which glowed with an otherworldly aura in the dark secret cavern of the bed. Her underwear soon followed. He pressed his naked body against hers from head to toe until he couldn't tell where he ended and she began. He didn't think he could survive if Nickie changed her mind.

"Griff?"

"I'm right here," he assured her as he slipped his arms around her and pressed his lower body against her. He kept himself propped on his elbows so he wouldn't be distracted by her soft breasts brushing his chest. He wanted to concentrate fully on experiencing the initial entry into her body. He was going to take it nice and slow, savoring every delicious inch, giving Nickie the chance to adjust to the feel of him inside her.

The mere thought sent a lightning surge of energy across the backs of his thighs, and he found himself thrusting instinctively against her until he was able to slip inside. He had to grit his teeth to keep from losing control immediately, and he only just managed it by thinking of Nickie's needs. He closed his eyes and groaned as he was completely enveloped in her heat.

"You okay?" he managed to ask.

"Oh, yes," she breathed.

She wrapped her arms around his torso and her legs around his hips, pulling him farther inside than he thought possible. He finally, blissfully, let go of the reins of control, making sure to take Nickie along with him every step of the way. How could she not follow him to ecstasy when he knew he was giving her the pure distilled essence of everything he was and could ever hope to be?

When she cried out, his own world shattered and he followed her seconds later.

He didn't want to let go when the first stirrings of outside awareness came. He lay on top of her, holding some of his weight away from her as best he could in his sated condition. He wanted to shout with triumph and kiss her with all the tenderness welling up inside him. He bent closer to kiss her closed eyelids, her nose, her cheeks.

"Oh, Griff," she whispered as she returned his kisses. "Let's stay enchanted as long as we possibly can."

"That sounds good to me."

He felt that they should always stay that way, but he knew instinctively not to say it. Instead, he rolled onto his back and pulled Nickie into his arms. His body was boneless, warm and contented. He pulled the sheet over them and soon heard Nickie's soft even breathing.

Maybe this place *was* magic, he thought, drawing a deep breath, unable to recall if he'd been breathing on a regular basis since they'd finished making love. Right now he didn't have the energy to argue with her assessment of Bellefleur's charm, not when he felt her murmuring in contentment and snuggling closer to him in the depths of her sleep.

She had somehow become the center of his world. When he wasn't with her, he found himself thinking about her all the time. She was smart and pretty and sexy. She responded to him as no other woman had, and she certainly caused nuclear meltdown in him.

The problem was, would he be able to keep her once he walked out the gates of Bellefleur?

NICKIE AWOKE MUCH LATER to find herself wrapped in Griff's arms.

Immediately her thoughts crowded in on her, as if they'd been waiting for her full attention. She realized she hadn't cared about anything but Griff during those magic moments when they were loving each other. She couldn't quite explain it, but it was almost as if she'd been encased in a magic cocoon that didn't allow the admission of doubts or fears. It had felt like a fairy tale where no matter how dire the situation became, things always turned out okay just in time for the happily ever after.

She caught a glimpse of the photo on her nightstand. It shimmered in the pale moonlight filtering through the sheer curtains that lifted in the breeze. She didn't have to actually see the details to know exactly how she looked as she stood on the porch steps of Bellefleur, her awkward legs encased in faded yellow shorts, her feet in scuffed sneakers. It wasn't much to look at, but that picture represented her lifelong dream.

She snuggled closer to Griff. No, she wasn't sorry. No woman could ever regret the wonderful experience he'd given her. But she knew she would have to pay the price all too soon. No matter what Griff said or promised, he would be leaving in a few days. She knew that he had the best intentions, that he truly believed they could keep the fires between them burning, but he didn't realize that distance had a way of defeating such ambitious plans.

She'd always been so careful about avoiding entanglements. Of course, those entanglements hadn't been with Griff. How could she resist him when she was falling in love with him? Already she couldn't imagine life at Bellefleur without him.

She only hoped that the ghost would be able to mend the shreds of her tattered heart once Griff had gone.

# Chapter Ten

Griff whistled cheerfully as he strode along the garden path, his mind still filled with the image of Nickie lying amid the rumpled sheets where he had just left her. He thought he should be commended for his stellar willpower. It hadn't been easy to leave her when all he wanted to do was spend the day in that four-poster bed. Still, he had to admit that a judicious period of rest would allow his body to recover from the effects of such prolonged lovemaking. It certainly wouldn't hurt his performance later.

The birds were out in full force this morning, singing their hearts out until he thought they would burst. He rounded the first corner, where the formal garden began as a border to the pathway, but the sight that greeted his eyes stopped him dead in his tracks.

The garden was lush and magnificent beyond his wildest dreams, like the enchanted garden of a fairy tale.

He heard an odd choking noise and realized to his consternation that he had produced it. He blinked once, thinking that he must be hallucinating or that he had wandered into the wrong garden, but the vision remained.

Had it only been three days since he'd cleared out the weeds in those flower beds? The struggling straggly begonias and geraniums had been doing their best, but the floral embroidery effect they were supposed to create had been thin and sketchy, revealing only remnants of their former loveliness beneath the months of neglect.

Now as he gazed at the thick, lush and stunningly brilliant red- and pink-hued rows of flowers that surrounded the box-tree scrolls, he couldn't believe what he was seeing. Had someone come in the night and filled in the curving design with more plants? The garden had always been beautiful, in spite of those areas where the lack of care had shown up first, but he couldn't remember it looking quite this way. Where on earth had this sudden lushness come from?

His eyes were wide open with disbelief and a small shiver crawled up his spine as he stood there gazing at the parterre. Was the rest of the place suddenly rejuvenated, as well? Almost afraid to check, he found himself walking slowly down the path, heading for the fountain.

Everywhere he looked, he swore he noticed changes, some so subtle he began to doubt his own senses. It must be his imagination. Admittedly, he didn't know an awful lot about the germination period of plants. Had the garden been so lacking in loving care that it had rewarded him by blossoming like this after only a few days' labor? Was it physically possible? Of course it had to be. He was sure Nickie would say it had something to do with the ghost, but in his mind, there had to be some scientific explanation.

He crossed the diagonal path, passing in front of the hillside in which sat embedded the statue of Apollo attended by nymphs. A small stream bubbled down the incline ending in a small pool where he could see several carp lazily swimming in the brown-tinted water.

In spite of his wishes to the contrary, he could feel the magic of the place enveloping him in a gentle caress, just as his grandfather had insisted. He wondered if he wasn't becoming as vulnerable to suggestion as his grandfather and Nickie. It was a sobering thought, and one he didn't care to dwell on.

He had simply forgotten what the garden looked like in the light of day. His night with Nickie was coloring everything else in his world. Maybe the investigation of kings and aristocrats had gone to his head. No doubt he would be okay after he got to work and finished the rest of the garden.

He decided he needed some good old-fashioned physical labor before he lost it completely. He quickly grabbed a broom and began sweeping the pathway, clearing it of the leaves and other debris that had gathered along the edges, especially at the crosswalks.

But he couldn't keep the smile from his face.

THE NEXT DAY was a time of enchantment for Nickie. She was suddenly doing the best work of her life, flying through the sketches of lizards and snakes and turtles as if her pencil had been taken over by Leonardo da Vinci.

That evening Nickie waited impatiently for Griff. He returned to the house around dusk, sweaty and tired, but as soon as he saw her, his face came alive in a way she would remember for the rest of her life. After dinner they drifted outside to the front porch and from there it was only natural to continue into the gardens for a stroll.

They talked and laughed amidst the lush greenery. Nickie breathed in the wonderful full-bodied scent of the flowers, their thick blossoms announcing that spring was quietly slipping into summer. There was nothing except the present. She wouldn't allow it any other way.

When they returned to the house, he took her in his arms and made love to her through the night until they both fell asleep in exhaustion. If she'd thought their first encounter was magic, she hadn't counted on it getting better.

In fact, it improved with each passing day, as every time they made love she learned how to best please him and he learned to increase her pleasure a hundred-fold.

She hadn't seen the ghost in days, but there could be two reasons for that state of affairs. Now that they knew his identity, perhaps he didn't feel the urge to haunt, if you could call his gentle presence a haunting. And secondly, she was with Griff almost all the time now, and unless the ghost wanted to appear to her in the bathroom, his chances of finding her alone were virtually nonexistent.

After the first morning she had taken to bringing her work materials into the garden and doing her sketches there. There was no doubt in her mind that it brought out the best of her talent, and besides, Griff usually took his shirt off by ten o'clock so she got to watch the play of muscle beneath his smooth skin as he stooped and raked and clipped.

She knew this magic state was temporary. It would have to end when Griff left in two days, just as things always ended. Although she wasn't sure if she would survive intact, she continued to assure herself that it was better to make a clean cut than to attempt to prolong their relationship.

It was close to lunchtime on the third morning of what she had come to think of as their enchanted interlude. She was sitting on one of the carved marble benches in the garden, working on a sketch of a glass lizard. Griff was busy trimming and shaping the low line of hedges that bordered the path up ahead.

She was beginning to feel restless. She could see that the gardens were almost restored. Only the farthest reaches, where the look was supposed to be naturally wild, had been untouched by Griff's capable hands. He was almost finished, which meant they were almost finished, too. She was trying her best to keep thoughts of the short time remaining out of her mind, but it was becoming more difficult with each passing minute.

She looked down and realized she'd forgotten a favorite tray of colored pencils. She had to keep working; therein lay the key to her sanity. Her work and Bellefleur were the only anchors that kept her world from flying apart at the seams.

"Griff," she called.

He turned to look over his shoulder at her, and the intimate expression that came into his eyes was almost her undoing. His smile was slow and sexy, and gathered impact as it spread across his face. "What can I do for you, Nickie?" he asked in a low seductive voice. The clippers now dangled unheeded at his side, since his intense focus had shifted from gardening to her.

"Um . . . I forgot some of my pencils. I'm going to run back and fetch them."

"Need any help?"

Her breath caught in her throat as her eyes met his and read the clear message there. He wanted her, wanted to make love to her again. This was something new. Neither of them had allowed their lovemaking to encroach on what could be considered working hours; it was an unspoken agreement between them. He must be realizing, as she was, that the time remaining for them to be together was quickly running out.

She longed to say yes. And yet all morning, in spite of her best efforts, a part of her had already begun quietly withdrawing, a self-protective measure against the final parting. She realized it was silly to waste the time they did have worrying about the inevitable, but that was the way it always seemed to work. Only in the all-encompassing dark of night, as she lay in the four-poster bed with Griff, could she forget.

She smiled, but it was a shaky effort. "I think I can manage."

He glanced at his watch, the only adornment on his entire perspiration-slicked gorgeous upper body. "Isn't it almost time for lunch?"

"Yes, I guess it is. I'll make us some sandwiches."

"And I'll be there as soon as I finish up this last bit." He grinned, but the look in his eyes promised more discussion on the subject. "Don't start without me."

"I wouldn't dream of it," she assured him.

She hurried along the path toward the house, biting her lip to keep her tears at bay. *Don't think, don't think,* she chanted silently to the rhythm of her feet hitting the ground. *Don't let yourself fall apart until he's gone.*

Bellefleur stood in the bright sunlight like a port in a storm and she rushed inside to the haven it offered. It was an illusion, however. There could be no safe haven in a house whose every room was stamped with memories of Griff. She gave herself a stern mental shake and forced her thoughts to shut down until further notice. Whether they would obey was another matter.

She quickly dashed up the stairs, thinking she would retrieve the errant pencils before starting lunch. She had them tucked under her arm as she barreled out of the study and almost careered into Audubon.

"Oh!" she gasped, stopping dead in her tracks.

He stood a few feet away, looking as elegant as usual. His coat this morning was green worn over a matching striped waistcoat, and his trousers were a lovely soft fawn. Part of the coat sleeve was opened with buttons to show off the ruffles at his wrist. His cravat had been tied in a simple bow, and there were pleats on his shirtfront. She wondered if he had to get dressed every day and, if so, where his wardrobe was stashed.

He looked agitated, but he managed a graceful bow.

She smiled at his strict observance of the proprieties. There could be no doubt he'd been raised a gentleman. She felt more at ease with him than ever before, even though her heart still skipped a couple of beats and her breathing grew shallow with excitement.

She managed to find her voice right away this time. "Good morning, Mr. Audubon."

She expected him to show amazement at her sudden and knowledgeable use of his name. She at least figured his eyebrows would shoot up in cool gentlemanly shock at what she considered her and Griff's skilled sleuthing.

That was not the reaction she got. Instead, he gestured frantically, indicating that he wanted her to follow him.

She sighed, then nodded. "All right, I'll follow you."

He half-floated, half-walked along the corridor. In fact, she couldn't figure out exactly how he was making his way ahead of her. He kept anxiously looking back over his shoulder to be sure she was behind him. She smiled back encouragingly.

He led her past the Rose Room, past the room where Griff was no longer sleeping by himself and straight to the portrait gallery. This was where she had come in search of artists' signatures several days ago. She stepped over the threshold just behind Audubon, who drifted in with those smooth ghostly motions of his, and gazed around in curiosity.

Her first thought was that he wanted to show her one of his paintings, although she couldn't remember seeing anything with his signature the afternoon she'd

searched. The ornately framed portraits of famous
and not-so-famous faces were interspersed with
soothingly delicate landscapes, mostly of the early
French school and done in the style of Watteau, which
meant that they were all painted before 1800. They
weren't necessarily of the first rank in execution, but
they were valuable nonetheless.

Audubon crossed immediately to the wall that dis-
played a line of likenesses of the Bourbon kings and
their families from the time of Louis the Pious right
up through poor doomed Louis XVI. To Nickie's
surprise, he drifted over to Louis XVI and pointed to
the bewigged monarch, looking at Nickie with his appealing eyes.

"What are you trying to say? Did you paint this
picture?" She leaned forward to peer in the corner for
a signature.

Obviously not, for he shooed her away with another graceful but emphatic gesture. He patted the air
in front of him in a motion that clearly bid her to be
still while he thought it over. Nickie waited quietly, a
puzzled frown wrinkling her forehead as her mind fe-
verishly worked to figure out what he might be trying
to communicate.

After a minute, he threw up his hands as if to say,
"aha!" before walking gracefully over to a portrait of
Louis XIV.

Nickie had noticed this painting before, because it
had been one of her favorites as a child. It didn't por-
tray the famous monarch in his middle age, wearing a
powdered wig and a haughty expression. This was
a likeness of the young sovereign, looking regally
handsome with his flowing brown locks and long

aristocratic nose with an appealing bump at the bridge.

Louis was wearing some sort of armor, and yet a delicate lace collar offset the harsh masculinity of his battle attire. His eyes glowed with that soft, limpid expression that paintings often imbued on their subjects, and his chiseled lips appeared about to break into a smile. In short, he was everything a young king should be.

This time Audubon gestured more emphatically, first indicating the painting, then pointing at himself. Nickie's eyes widened as she voiced the thought uppermost in her mind.

"Are you trying to tell me you're related to these people?"

He nodded vigorously.

"But how?"

Before he could resort to the tedious process of more sign language, the sound of the front door banging against the wooden frame brought both of them up short.

"Nickie," Griff shouted in a cheerful voice. "Where are you?"

"Oh, please, don't go," she begged the ghost, stretching out a pleading hand.

"Nickie! Are you upstairs?"

She turned toward the doorway. "Yes. Just hang on a minute, I'll be right down," she called.

When she looked back, Audubon had vanished.

"Damn," she muttered, but she couldn't manage to muster up a lot of indignation, not when Audubon had just provided another clue to a mystery they had thought neatly solved. Could it possibly be true? Had her imperious aunt been correct all along? Nickie took a last lingering glance at young Louis, then hurried from the room.

Griff met her just as she stepped onto the interfloor landing. "I was getting lonely down here," he told her with a wicked grin. He pulled her into his arms. "What took you so long?"

She slipped one arm around his neck. "Nothing much," she replied with an airy wave of her free hand. But then she spoiled the nonchalant effect by chuckling. Either her diluted French blood was beginning to tell after all this time, or she was picking up the ghost's habit of using his hands as an eloquent and expressive substitute for verbal conversation. "Audubon wanted to tell me something."

"You saw him again?" Griff's hands tightened as they gripped her waist. For a brief moment she thought he was going to push her aside, but he merely slipped them behind her back and continued to hold her in a loose embrace. "Tell me."

"Okay. But you'd better prepare yourself."

She smiled into his eyes, suddenly realizing how wonderful it was having Griff here to share this adventure as he now shared her body and even her soul. Her face must have reflected her thoughts, because he seemed to read the change immediately, bending his head to kiss her. It was a long lingering kiss that gave much and promised much more. Her entire body softened with pleasure at the gently insistent pressure of his mouth and the delicious warmth generated by their intermingled breaths.

He ended the kiss as tenderly as he'd begun it. The expression in his eyes was a heady mixture of potent desire and masculine indulgence. He would yield both the pace and the ghost to her.

She rubbed her face against his shirt, breathing in his warm clean scent. "That wasn't quite what I meant when I said prepare yourself."

"Sure you did," he murmured, kissing the crown of her head. "Now you're the one who's stalling. I'm just waiting here for you to tell me."

"Yeah, until Sunday," she reminded him tartly, the mood suddenly shattered as she remembered they had such a short time left together.

"Yes, but I'll be back. Or maybe you can come visit me in California."

"I've heard that before."

"But not from me." He turned her firmly around, sliding an arm across her shoulders and leading her down the last flight of stairs. "Now tell me what Audubon said. Or how he gestured with his elegant hands and implied with his expressive eyes."

She eyed him suspiciously as they squeezed through the kitchen door together. "Are you just humoring me, or do you really believe me about the ghost?"

"I have to believe you Nickie, because I've fallen in love with you."

She pulled away and whirled to confront him. She could feel tears beginning to form in her eyes, and it took everything she possessed to quell them. "Don't say that. Don't make things harder than they already are."

He drew back, a hurt expression flickering across his handsome features. She watched him clench his jaw to control it, but traces of the pain of her rejection were still visible in his eyes. She had never seen anything like that there before, and she realized he had become vulnerable to her. She wasn't the only one whom this relationship was going to hurt. Oh, why had she ever allowed it to get started in the first place? She knew better!

She reached out a hand to him, but he didn't move to take it. "Let's not change anything," she said. "Let's just keep things the way they are."

"The way they are is that I'm in love with you. Not saying it isn't going to change anything."

"Please." She met his gaze and her expression pleaded for his agreement. She wasn't above resorting to sobbing and begging, not when his answer could mean the difference between a possible hold on sanity or a total breakdown after he left. She only hoped she wouldn't have to use such tactics.

He turned away and walked over to the window. It appeared to be a perfectly natural action, except that his hands gripped the window ledge so tightly the skin on his knuckles lost all color.

"If it makes you feel better, I won't mention it again," he told her over his shoulder in a flat low-pitched voice. "Anything not to distress a lady."

She swallowed hard against the lump in her throat. "Thank you."

"Isn't that how your friend Audubon would handle it?"

"Um . . . yes, I suppose he would."

He crossed the room to tower over her, grabbing her upper arms and forcing her to meet his angry stare. "Just remember one thing, Nickie. I might have promised not to say the words aloud, but I'll be thinking them and feeling them while I'm making love to you tonight. And that means you will, too—I intend to make sure you do.''

His words sent a surge of excitement and dismay racing through her. She couldn't look away.

''After that, if you still want to throw away what we've found together, I won't stop you.''

He released her arms abruptly and went to sit at the table. Nickie automatically rubbed her skin with cold fingers, although he hadn't hurt her.

''All right, that's settled,'' he said. ''Now let's get back to what you were trying to tell me about the ghost.''

''Okay.'' She smiled in an effort to act as if this abrupt refocusing of their dialogue was the most normal thing in the world. She didn't think she succeeded very well, but Griff appeared to be in a more tolerant frame of mind than when he'd grabbed her arms. His expression had softened from grimness to blankness as he waited for her to speak.

After the shock of his revelation, she could hardly remember that Bellefleur even had a ghost, never mind what had just happened in the portrait gallery. All she knew for sure was that Griff didn't seem like the kind of man who said, ''I love you,'' just because he thought it was expected. She figured he said it because he meant it, and that meant trouble for her. She quickly forced herself to gather her thoughts.

''Yes, the ghost. Audubon.'' She opened the refrigerator as if deciding what to have for lunch, but it was really an attempt to buy herself a little time to restore the calm she needed. ''He was somehow related to Louis XIV. Or Louis XVI. I'm not sure exactly what he was trying to imply, but there's definitely some connection between him and one of those kings."

"How do you know?"

She quickly explained what had happened and how Audubon had pointed out the portraits to her. The more she spoke about the ghost, the more normal she began to feel. It was ironic that now the ghost made her feel normal, and Griff caused her insides to turn into a roiling mass of confusion.

When she finished, Griff looked thoughtful. "We need more information on Audubon's background."

"Yeah, and we need the kind of stuff you don't find in the usual places. We should also try to find out if either of the kings had a son who disappeared or left the country."

"He may have been an illegitimate descendant."

"Yes, of course! An illegitimate son who could have been king, only he wasn't allowed to be a successor because of the circumstances of his birth. They were always such sticklers for things like that." Nickie felt a stirring of excitement and tried to concentrate on it to the exclusion of everything else. "That makes the most sense of anything we've come up with so far. After all, he was adopted. And by a Frenchman. There was nothing to tell where he'd been before that."

"How about the county library at Stoddard?" Griff said. "They might have more than Linton could provide, and it's only a twenty-minute drive."

"Great idea. I'll go there after lunch."

"I'll come, too. I've pretty much accomplished what I set out to do here."

Her heart fluttered at the thought of being with the man who claimed to love her. "Don't you trust my researching abilities?"

"More than ever," he said with a wicked smile. "I'm not about to let you spend an entire afternoon away from me. Besides, I don't think I can wait until later to hear what you find out."

She took a deep breath. "Then let's get going."

LESS THAN AN HOUR LATER they were seated at a worn wooden table scored with the initials of previous patrons. The reference section of the Stoddard County Regional Library wasn't large, but when they'd asked the librarian for help, she had returned with two stacks of sources. Nickie pounced on a thick biography of Audubon, while Griff opened a large encyclopedia about French history. They both began to read.

Half an hour later she leaned her elbows on the table in a dispirited fashion.

Griff glanced up. "What's the matter?" he whispered.

"Nothing really," she whispered back, even though there was no one else in that part of the library. "It's just that all these sources say the same thing—that Audubon was adopted by Jean Audubon at Les Cayes, Haiti, when he was about nine years old, and nothing more. Either they're all copying from each other, or they all simply don't have any more information and we're barking up the wrong tree. What have you found out?"

"Well, Louis XIV's descendants all seem to be accounted for. We already know that Louis XVI had a son, Louis Charles, who was kept prisoner during the

Reign of Terror. He's recorded as having died shortly after both his parents were executed, but there seems to be some mystery about the circumstances of his death. The trouble is, this source doesn't provide any concrete information."

"What kind of mystery?"

"I don't know. It just says here that some historians believe he didn't die, but was spirited away to one of the other royal courts in Europe. However, according to this, most reputable scholars consider the theory pure romantic speculation. Anyway, he's known as the Lost Dauphin."

"The Lost Dauphin," she repeated, her eyes narrowed. "Are there any pictures of him?"

"No."

She tapped her fingers against the open pages of the Audubon biography. "When was he born?"

"1785."

"You're kidding. That's when Audubon was born."

"It's probably just a coincidence."

"Maybe. When did he die?"

"Let's see . . . 1794."

She sucked in her breath and let it out with a slow hiss. "Audubon was adopted in 1794. In a French colony by a Frenchman."

"Are you trying to say that Audubon was the Lost Dauphin?" He frowned.

"Why not? It's as good a possibility as anything else we've come up with."

He chuckled. "Two coincidences, and she wants to rewrite the history books."

"Cut it out, Griff. I agree that we definitely need more to go on. And yet it's all starting to add up in a crazy sort of way." She began ticking off the items. "One, Bellefleur was built by émigré French royalists and is filled with portraits of French kings and queens. Two, Audubon was a frequent and honored guest according to that register we found. Three, everyone agrees there's some mystery surrounding the man's birth, even though they can't agree on what it is. And four, the gardens at Bellefleur were modeled on those at Versailles, where I presume the Lost Dauphin spent his childhood."

"You still haven't come up with anything concrete. Let's see what this last biography of Audubon has to say." Griff picked it up and began to peruse the index.

Nickie sat thoughtfully, trying to fit together the pieces of this puzzle she'd inherited with Bellefleur. She was sure they were on the right track. They just needed to dig a little deeper.

"Aha," Griff said.

"Aha what?" As she waited for Griff to explain, she idly reached for an old decrepit-looking volume the librarian had just deposited on the table, although her eyes didn't focus on the pages.

"Listen to this," Griff said. "'It has been suggested, most notably by Frances Cox Coakeley in her dubious 1902 biography, that the artist was actually the Lost Dauphin of France, although there are no facts to support this theory.'"

He stopped. Nickie waited for him to continue, but he simply sat there pondering the page in front of him. "Keep going," she urged him.

"That's it. It goes on from there with the usual party line about how most historians believe he was born at Les Cayes, Haiti, et cetera, et cetera."

"Oh," Nickie breathed reverently. "That's it then, it's true."

"What about the part that says there're no facts to support the theory?"

Nickie ignored him. Her gaze fell to the book in her hands, and she began leafing through it. "Oh, my gosh! Look at this." She poked the page with an eager finger as she spoke. "It says here that there's some indication that Audubon was adopted somewhere outside Paris during the French Revolution. That would definitely put him right in the thick of things. Oh, and look! Right here it says what you were just reading—that he was the lost Dauphin but that he never told anyone except his wife, and she was sworn to keep the secret."

Griff frowned. "What is that book?"

She quickly turned it over to peer at the spine, then grinned. "Frances Cox Coakeley's dubious biography."

"Hmm. She seems to be bucking the historical tide."

"So? That doesn't make her wrong." She clenched her hands into tight fists and brought one of them up to tap her chin impatiently. "This is so frustrating. All we have is one slim thread of conjecture and no proof. Where are we ever going to find out the truth?"

"What about that expert my grandfather mentioned, the one your aunt went to see?"

"Of course. That's when she came back all enthused about building the garden." It was Nickie's turn to frown. "Do you think she found out something concrete from this woman, or did she already have her mind so fixated on having a king in the house that nothing would dissuade her?"

"There's only one way to find out and that's to go see her."

# Chapter Eleven

Jean Haversoll lived on a tree-lined boulevard in one of the older suburbs of Memphis. Griff parked the car and came around to help Nickie out of the low-slung vehicle, his hand lingering on her shoulder in a gesture of possession and care that made her heart turn over. She'd known Griff would be devastating in bed, but she'd never imagined he would act this way out of it. The more he possessed her physically, the more intense his focus on her became.

"Well, let's go see what we can discover," he said cheerfully as he smiled down into her eyes. He was so open with her now she felt guilty. He was allowing her into his heart and soul, while she was trying to protect herself at all costs.

She quickly turned her thoughts to the interview ahead. Ms. Haversoll had come across as a gracious generous woman over the phone; she remembered Marie-Claire DuPrés very well and certainly hadn't expressed any surprise to hear from her grandniece. She had readily agreed to see both her and Griff.

They stepped onto the screened-in porch so they could knock on the front door. Ms. Haversoll had given her last exam yesterday and had papers to grade, but she had kindly consented to take time away from that. Nickie had the feeling the historian was more than a little interested to find out what they wanted.

The door opened to reveal a tall, rather beautiful woman in her late forties. Jean Haversoll had wavy red hair that framed her exotic high-cheekboned face, and she wore a green print dress that flattered her curvaceous body and brought out the green in her hazel eyes. She didn't look like any college professor Nickie had ever seen. She could imagine more than one smitten male student in her classes.

"Hi. You must be Nickie DuPrés. Come on in." She held open the door, speaking in a soft beguiling tone that held just the faintest hint of a Southern accent.

"Ms. Haversoll, this is a friend, Griff McInnis."

Griff nodded cordially. "It's a pleasure," he said, holding out his hand.

"Hello. And you must both call me Jean. I've heard Ms. Haversoll for an entire semester and it's time for a break."

She led them to a nicely furnished informal living room. Of course, Nickie thought with a faint smile, after Bellefleur, anything else was informal. They waited while Jean disappeared into the kitchen and returned with a pitcher of iced tea and some cookies arranged on a platter.

"Your great-aunt also came to ask me what I knew about the son of Louis XVI," she said as she poured the tea and handed them each a glass. "I must admit I'm very curious to discover if any other evidence has turned up."

"Evidence? What kind of evidence?"

She appeared puzzled. "Marie-Claire showed me the sketches, of course."

Nickie looked at Griff who simply shrugged, a smile on his face. *This is your show,* he seemed to be saying. He was prepared to let her handle it without interference. When she smiled back at him she could feel the special connection between them.

She turned to Jean again. "What sketches?" she asked.

"Why, the matching sketches of Louis XVI and Marie Antoinette." When she noticed Nickie's continued baffled expression she lifted elegant fingers to cover her lips in surprise and astonishment. "You don't know about them? Oh, dear, I hope nothing happened to them. They weren't sold, were they?"

"They couldn't have been. Nothing has been sold from Bellefleur since my great-aunt's time there."

"Thank goodness." Jean leaned forward in her chair. "They weren't very large, about five by seven inches I'd say. I tried to get Marie-Claire's permission to use them as illustrations. At the time I was working on a book about Louis XVI, but after what she told me I knew I couldn't continue without further research. It took me a couple of years to arrange it, but I finally managed to get away to France, stopping in Haiti along the way. I discovered some interesting information. But when I called her with my finds, she said the time wasn't right to reveal the secret."

Nickie's eyes glowed. "You mean about the identity of the Lost Dauphin?"

"Exactly. Do you know much about his life before he disappeared from history's view?"

"No."

"Then let me tell you the facts as I know them. You can decide for yourselves."

"Oh, yes, please," Nickie breathed. She could feel her palms tingling with excitement as she settled back to listen.

"The young dauphin, son of Louis XVI, was a handsome graceful boy who was educated as befitted a royal prince, even after his family was imprisoned. He was a bright child and excelled at many things. He played several instruments well enough to teach them professionally, even though he was only a boy, including the violin and flute."

"And the flageolet?" Nickie interrupted softly.

"And the flageolet," the older woman agreed with a smile.

Nickie's eyes met Griff's as another jolt of awareness shot through her.

Jean took a sip of her tea before continuing, a soft smile on her face. "He could draw and paint better than his tutors. And he was fluent in French, English and Spanish. He was also loaded with charm. Even his jailers couldn't resist him as they tried to keep him happy and entertained. One of his passions was a love of birds, and his captors allowed him to keep a few of them for company.

"Eventually a new couple, the Simons, replaced the original custodians. They also grew very fond of the boy and even had a large aviary placed by one of the windows. When they were abruptly fired a year later, no one inspected the big bundles of linen they carried out of the prison, along with their belongings."

She paused dramatically, allowing her gaze to search the faces of her listeners like any well-trained teacher.

Apparently satisfied that they had grasped the implications of her tale, she went on, "There is some evidence to indicate that when the dust settled the guards discovered the boy was missing. One account says they supposedly replaced the dauphin, who was technically now Louis XVII, with another little boy because they were afraid to reveal their laxness to their superiors. Within six months the child, whoever he was, was dead."

"If the Simons did smuggle the dauphin out, what happened to him?" Nickie asked.

"That's exactly what your aunt wanted to know. She wondered if the child might not have been spirited away to America. As I'm sure you know, she subscribed to a theory I had read about but one that I knew had long since been dismissed as utter nonsense. She believed that the boy became John James Audubon, the famous naturalist and bird specialist. I'll never forget how she calmly explained to me that it was all true."

"Did she tell you about the ghost of Bellefleur?" Nickie felt foolish asking, but she had to know.

"Yes, as a matter of fact, she did. Have you seen it, too?" Jean asked the question in a resigned tone of voice, neither incredulous nor condemning.

Nickie glanced over at Griff, who grinned back at her. She smiled and shrugged sheepishly. "Yes."

"He's been rather persistent about it," Griff added casually.

"Well, I consider myself a practical woman, so of course I had to dismiss her source. But I couldn't so easily ignore those sketches. They convinced me it wouldn't be a waste of time to search further. During my trip abroad, I checked the records. That's when I discovered that just forty-five days after the Simons departed, a man named Jean Audubon adopted a nine-year-old boy just outside Paris.''

Griff reached for Nickie's hand and gave it a squeeze. She held on tightly as she said, "Then it's true. Audubon *is* the Lost Dauphin."

"I believe he is. And this time I intend to write that book, with or without the sketches. Your great-aunt insisted that Audubon's accomplishments should stand on their own merit, that he didn't need any further glossing. Of course that's true, he made his mark on history, but I can see no harm in revealing his secret now, and I ask again for your permission to use those drawings Audubon made of his parents."

Nickie's smile was warm. "My immediate instinct is to say yes, provided we find them, naturally, but let me take a little time think about it."

"Of course." Jean rose from her seat and began picking up the empty glasses. "You can't stop the tide of history, Nickie. These things always come out one way or another."

"DO YOU THINK this is what Audubon wants, for his secret to be told?" Nickie asked Griff as they drove through the gates of Bellefleur and past the gardener's cottage.

"Why not?" Griff said, downshifting into the curve of the driveway. "He certainly went to a lot of trouble to tell you about his origins."

"But why now?"

"Again, why not?" He parked in his usual place beneath the tree, then turned to face her, his green eyes gleaming with humor. "It makes as much sense as anything else about this does."

She blew out her breath. "Then I'll do it. I'll let Jean Haversoll use the sketches. If we can find them." She paused in the action of reaching for the door handle, her expression thoughtful. "I wonder if maybe they're in the attic. It's the only place I haven't looked, although I can't imagine why Marie-Claire would want to put two extremely valuable drawings up there."

"So let's check it out."

They climbed the stairs from the second floor to the attic. Nickie flipped on the lights. The place smelled dry and dusty, and the air felt hot and stuffy.

They stood for a few moments to let their eyes adjust to the gloom which the overhead lighting did little to alleviate. In fact, the fixtures appeared as dusty as everything else, and the light had to penetrate a layer of dirt.

"Look." Nickie pointed. "There's that old rocking horse. I sneaked up here and rode it, but it creaked so loudly that Marie-Claire found me and forbade me to return."

Griff lifted his brows. "Maybe she had something to hide."

"Maybe. But not in this section," she said, gazing around at the battered trunks and the cobwebs that hung in every corner and decorated the dismantled bedstead standing off to one side. "Let's check in the next room. I'd rather not start poking around in here unless we have to."

She glanced down at her feet, then at the surrounding floor where they'd left a trail of fresh footprints in the thick dust. She suddenly realized that a fairly dust-free pathway led from the stairs directly to the inner room of the attic. She started to mention as much to Griff, but she saw that he'd already noticed.

"It looks as though your aunt must have come here on a regular basis."

Nickie carefully pushed open the door and peered inside. The lone window at the end of the room did little to light their way, so she flicked on the wall switch and gazed around.

It was a small room that contained an old rolltop desk, a chair and a filing cabinet on which was piled a stack of faded black ledgers. The top of the desk was clear except for an ugly green goosenecked lamp, but the cubbyholes appeared stuffed with papers. Nickie's stomach fluttered as she imagined the information that might be stored there.

"Bingo. We just hit pay dirt," Griff said behind her. He wrapped his arms around her neck and across her collarbone, pulling her back against his body and turning her toward the west wall in the same motion.

Nickie leaned back against him, crossing her arms over his and resting her hands on his forearms as she gazed ahead. There they were, the two sketches, hanging smugly in the center of the wall. Beneath them sat one of the small delicate tables that so suited the decor of Bellefleur. And on the table sat a buckram-covered book, propped on an easel. The entire effect was like that of a shrine.

Nickie moved closer. Griff kept the contact and moved right along with her. She could see Louis on the left and Marie Antoinette on the right. The background in both pictures showed only enough traces of an ugly cracked stone wall and a window with thick metal bars to leave the viewer in no doubt about the location. The pair were dressed simply, yet they seemed more noble than if they had been clothed in the finest silks and furs. The knowledge of their fate showed starkly on their care-ravaged faces and in their eyes.

Down in the corner, just above Audubon's signature on the portrait of Marie Antoinette, the words *Chère Maman* had been penned in an elaborate cursive script. The label on the drawing of Louis was a simple eloquent *Papa*.

"No wonder Jean Haversoll was so convinced by these drawings," Nickie commented softly.

She held tightly to Griff. They stood there in silence for several long moments before she spoke again in the hushed whisper that seemed suitable in the face of such revelations of history. "Of course my aunt put them here. She knew how fascinated I was by the attic when I was a child, and probably figured I couldn't resist coming up here as soon as I got back." She half sighed, half chuckled. "Little did she realize that the family ghost was just as eager for me to learn the secret as she was."

"What's the book?" Griff asked.

She reached for the small volume, holding it up so he could read the faded lettering on the spine. "Frances Cox Coakeley. Who else?"

He grinned as he nuzzled her neck. "The dubious lady biographer sure gets around." He kissed the side of her head.

"Yeah, but now she's having the last laugh."

"She deserves it." He released his hold on her so he could take her hand. "Come on."

She remained staring at the sketches. "We should take them downstairs and hang them in the portrait gallery."

"It can wait until tomorrow. Right now we have more important things to do."

She didn't have to ask what he meant before she caught a glimpse of the heavy desire in his eyes. It sparked an immediate response that flooded her body like liquid fire even as a sharp pain filled her heart. Everything could wait until tomorrow, because that's when Griff had to leave.

She made no protest when he tugged on her hand to lead her from the attic. His fingers were warm as they held hers, his grip firm. He pulled her through the doorway at the bottom of the stairs, closing the door with a push of his foot. Then he backed her up against the wall, flattening her body with the urgent weight of his as he lowered his mouth to kiss her.

Nickie felt her knees buckle as she went limp with desire. She automatically clutched at his shoulders, but he was already supporting her, using the wall to keep her upright and his right leg to stop her from sliding to the floor. She ached where the hard muscles of his thigh pressed against the most vulnerable part of her.

He tasted good. His mouth, as it slanted across hers searching for more contact, generated so much heat she thought they would both burst into flame. His hands roamed restlessly up and down her sides, stopping to fondle her breasts, shaping the curve of her hips and squeezing her bottom.

"This is our last night together, Nickie," he said when he finally tore his mouth away. His breath was warm against the skin of her neck.

"Yes."

It was the only answer she could manage. She wasn't sure she ever wanted to recover from the onslaught of his drugging kisses. The force of his powerful will surrounded her, mixed with the very air she was pulling into her lungs in small, gasping breaths.

He scooped her into his arms and strode down the hallway to her bedroom. "I want you to know right now that I plan on making the most of it," he said as he carried her over the threshold. "I know as soon as I walk out that door tomorrow, you're going to tell yourself that the most sensible thing do is to push me out of your mind."

He set her down in the middle of the room, then started backing her the rest of the way toward the big old-fashioned bed. When the mattress finally stopped their inexorable progress, he was ready. He caught her up in his arms and tossed her onto the covers, vaulting immediately after her and rolling on top of her before she knew what had happened.

"I'm not going to let you push me out of your mind, Nickie," he told her, speaking in that low intense voice that turned her insides to jelly.

She didn't argue with him about it. There'd be time enough for that later, along with a flood of regrets. And yet in spite of what she knew about human nature, his words were stirring her blood as nothing else in her life ever had. She loved hearing them, even though she realized Griff was saying them in the heat of passion, a passion that could never exist in such a pure unadulterated form once it was severed by distance.

Reaching down, he pulled her shirt over her head and unfastened and pushed aside her bra. Then he stroked his hand across her breast, catching her nipple deliciously in his palm, circling and rubbing until she thought she would scream from the pleasure.

"Do you like that, Nickie?" he rasped. "Tell me you like it."

She whimpered, a sound that could almost be mistaken for pain, although both of them knew better. "Griff, please," she begged with a sob.

She wasn't sure exactly what she was pleading for, although she knew it had something to do with hoping he wouldn't make it any more difficult for her, that he would let her go. And yet she prayed that he would keep her pinned to the bed forever, so that this night would never end.

His next words revealed that he must have read something of her confused thoughts in her eyes. "Oh, no, I'm not going to make it easy for you by going quietly."

She swallowed hard as he resumed his sensual assault on her body. She knew that this night was now irrevocably in Griff's hands; he sensed it, too. Tonight she would yield everything to him, because her heart and her body wouldn't allow her to do otherwise.

He moved aside so he could strip the rest of the clothes from her body. While she watched with glazed hungry eyes, he rid himself of his own clothes. Their eyes met as he tossed the last item aside, and a jolt of such longing to be joined with him passed through her it almost lifted her off the bed.

"You might as well know my plan," he said as he slid his body along the length of hers, making sure she experienced every inch of his bare flesh. "It's no real secret."

He grasped her hands and pinned them next to her head, crushing her breasts with the restrained weight of his body. When she finally met his gaze and he was sure he had her complete attention, he spoke again. "I'm going to make love to you so thoroughly you're not going to know what hit you. I intend to burn myself into every fiber of your being until I'm sure you'll never forget me."

She caught her breath at the intensity of his expression. His gaze continued to bore into her, scorching her very soul with the undeniable strength of his will.

"And then," he concluded with a feral growl, brushing his mouth softly against hers as he spoke, "and then I'll be back to make sure of it."

Nickie never even noticed when the quickening darkness outside the window finally lost all trace of daylight. She had been swept away on a whirlwind of pleasure, cocooned in the darkness of the huge canopy bed, outside of time and place. The only sounds to be heard were the groans of pleasure they made.

Griff certainly kept his word, not that she had ever doubted he would. He loved her all night long, barely stopping after one pinnacle before forging ahead in search of the next.

WHEN SHE OPENED her eyes the next morning, the first thing she saw was Griff, standing naked by the window. The strong proud planes of his back and the muscled lines of his thighs reminded her of one of the classic Greek statues that lined the walkways in Bellefleur's garden. Zeus without the beard. She smiled at the notion, but decided it wasn't all that far off, not when she could still feel the aftereffects of last night in various key places of her body.

She stretched languidly, pulling the sheet up to shield herself against the faint chill that lingered in the morning air. She had no idea what time it was, but she could hear the ubiquitous birds singing, although she couldn't see any in the branches that were visible through the window. A single shaft of sunlight illuminated the windowsill next to Griff's elbow.

He turned around, his gaze snagging hers immediately, even though she was lying at the farthest reach of the bed beneath the shadowy canopy. A slow beautiful smile spread across his face. She had never seen him smile like that. Every trace of self-control, every hard emotion, was gone, as was the powerful determination he called forth so easily to help him handle the problems of life. She knew her own expression was soft, probably even wistful, as she smiled back.

"Everything is flowering out there. It's the damnedest thing. It seems that ever since I arrived here there's been an invisible force at work." He glanced back out the window, running his fingers through the rumpled waves of his dark hair. "I swear I must be losing my mind, but I can't get rid of the feeling that all this lush abundance at Bellefleur is somehow connected to our growing feelings for each another, like it's some kind of physical manifestation of them."

He strode unabashedly to the bed, leaning across its vast breadth to grasp her hand. His fingers were warm as they curled around hers. His eyes were very green this morning and he looked happy. "As you can see, you've gone to my head. One night of mind-blowing lovemaking leaves me prey to all kinds of whimsical notions."

"So I see."

"Do you?" His eyes narrowed as he stared into her face. He continued to toy casually with her fingers, but she wasn't fooled. He wasn't going to avoid things, not even for a minute. It shouldn't have surprised her when he handled everything else head-on. She had hoped to bathe in the afterglow just a while longer before facing the harsh glare of reality.

"I thought you might try to say that what happened between us last night was only sex." He held up her hand, measuring it against the greater width and breadth of his. "But it wasn't, was it, Nickie?"

Her fingers twitched nervously against his palm. Oh, God, the moment had come, and much more quickly than she wanted. She wasn't prepared. She still felt too soft and emotional, too sated to be able to deal with what had to be done for both their sakes.

"It was wonderful," she replied. She could feel the beginning of tears welling up in the corners of her eyes, but she clenched her jaw against them, forcing them back. "And now you're leaving."

She sensed that his entire body stilled, like a great wary, watching cat. "So?"

"So we probably won't see each other again, or if we do, it won't be the same."

"Is that right?" he asked, and his voice was harsh with sarcasm.

She couldn't meet his penetrating gaze so she dropped her head. "Yes," she whispered, her voice barely audible. She cleared her throat and tried to speak louder, although it was difficult to get past the lump in her throat. "So why don't we just agree to say goodbye now, make a clean break. That way we can remember how good it was and not how our feelings faded from the heights of passion to an annual Christmas card with a little note in it."

He pushed himself off the bed and stalked to his pants, which were lying on the floor where he had blindly tossed them last night. With quick jerky movements, he pulled them over his lean hips.

"I can't believe you're really going to do this." He glanced around angrily, looking for his shirt and finally locating it tangled around a post at the foot of the bed. He grabbed it, holding it bunched in both fists, and glared at her. "I'll be the first one to admit that trying to conduct a long-distance relationship is not the easiest thing in the world. I realize you want to stay here at Bellefleur. Right now I've got a job in California. But after that, who knows?"

She frowned. "Are you saying you're willing to give up your work just to stay here?"

"I don't know. I haven't thought it through that far yet. I just know that I love you and that I don't happen to fall in love every day. I'm not going to kill it off now, just in case it doesn't work out later."

"It has to be this way," she insisted stubbornly. "You'll see that I'm right once you get to California.

You'll be glad you didn't try to tie yourself to a relationship that has no future.''

"We can't know that for sure unless we try it.'' He held up his hand as she was about to speak. "I know, I know. You've already tried it and it doesn't work. But dammit, that wasn't us, Nickie.'' He glanced down at the crumpled shirt with a frown, shaking it out and then thrusting his arms into the sleeves. "Get dressed. I can't think straight when you're lying there like that.''

She felt like burying her head under the pillows until Griff left, but she began a halfhearted attempt to find her clothes. Obviously she wasn't moving fast enough to suit him because he snatched some of her things from the floor beside the bed and tossed them to her.

"I thought you had courage,'' he said in low-voiced accusation. His eyes were filled with helpless frustration as he clenched his fists at his sides.

She slid off the edge of the bed, standing on the far side so that the high mattress was between them as she began putting on her clothes. "You don't think it takes courage to end things now, before they can get any worse?''

"How does love get worse, will you tell me that?'' He kicked one of his shoes into the middle of the floor. "And by the way, I think it takes cowardice to end things now, not courage.''

She knew it was useless to argue with him about it. He didn't want to see the plain facts in front of his nose, but they remained there in spite of his blindness—there was no future for them. She had promised herself she would never return to the kind of vagabond life she had worked so hard all these years to reject. When she'd asked him point-blank about his solution to their dilemma, his response had been a revealing "I don't know." It was obvious she couldn't count on changing him.

"I can't talk to you. You've obviously made up your mind, and nothing I say is going to change it." He walked around the edge of the bed so that all that stood between them were their differences. "I've bought you a plane ticket to Los Angeles," he said in a quiet voice. "Things will be too hectic at first for me to get away, but that doesn't mean *you* can't come out for a weekend."

"Los Angeles?" She felt an unexpected thrill of excitement crawl up her spine. Golden California, land of sunshine and computers, the cutting edge of American culture. She'd never been there. She immediately scolded herself. What was she doing, allowing herself to get caught up in the adventure of travel, even for a moment? She'd already traveled enough to last a lifetime.

"You just need to call the airline and tell them which day you want to leave."

With those words he turned on his heel and walked to the door. But he wasn't through with her yet. He paused in the doorway, swiveling his head only enough to be able to speak to her over his shoulder. "I believed in your ghost without proof. Why can't you believe in me enough to know I'll figure a way out of this?"

She remained where she was, standing by the bed with one hand resting on the sheets where they had so recently loved each other. She felt stunned, numb. Although she wasn't facing the door, she knew when Griff left the room. Somehow she couldn't open her mouth to call him back. She couldn't move, but she realized she couldn't just stand there forever. Finally she roused herself enough to search for some clean clothes and head for the shower.

It seemed a small eternity had passed when she emerged from the shower, unrefreshed and still numb. She listened carefully but she didn't hear any noise coming from Griff's room. She didn't imagine it would take him long to pack, but she didn't have the courage to check if he was still there.

Instead, she returned to her room, her gaze averted from the bed. She realized now that it had been a mistake to make love with Griff there. Now she would think of him every time she slept. She had the sinking feeling she would be thinking of him all the time, period.

The noise of the front door closing drew her to the window. She didn't want to, but she found herself leaning forward, gazing through the screen to watch him walk down the driveway to his car. If he knew she was there, he didn't bother to glance up, but instead, threw his bag onto the passenger seat and got into the car. She heard the engine come to life even as her own life force felt as though it was draining out of her body and into the carpet at her feet.

Now that he couldn't possibly see her, she pressed her face to the glass, straining to catch a last glimpse of him through the trees as he drove down the street. A flash of silver-green was her only reward and then he was gone.

Quietly she began to cry.

# Chapter Twelve

Nickie sat disconsolately at her desk, toying with a gum eraser and staring glumly at the blank sheet of paper in front of her. Two weeks had passed since Griff had walked out the door, fourteen of the longest, most miserable days she'd ever spent. Even the brilliant summer sun slanting in through the tall windows and the sound of twittering birds filtering through the screen couldn't lift her spirits.

She hadn't seen Audubon since that time, either. It seemed to her that the bird population of Bellefleur had thinned out considerably without his presence. She told herself that it all made sense, that they had solved the mystery of his origins and his ghostly soul could now be at peace; he no longer had to roam the halls of Bellefleur. Nevertheless, she couldn't help feeling depressed. The two men had simultaneously entered her life and simultaneously departed.

Still, Audubon could have at least come to say goodbye.

Now she felt deserted, abandoned, in spite of having made the bottom-line choice that had thrust her into these circumstances. Her appetite was nonexistent. She had trouble falling asleep because memories assailed her. And once she was asleep, she had trouble waking up, as if her body wanted to slumber forever, like Rip Van Winkle, in the slim hope of awakening to better times. As if all that wasn't bad enough, she found her work was suffering, and that was something she had to find a way to change.

She poked halfheartedly at the stack of pencils in front of her. The old cliché about grief and sorrow producing great art was certainly proving to be a falsehood. In her case, it seemed that happiness made for productivity. Her artistic faculties had dried up the moment Griff had walked out of her life. Without him the well had become empty, and she wasn't sure if she could ever fill it again.

What good was a beautiful property where she could put down roots if she had no one to share it with, she thought for the umpteenth time as she gazed around the beautiful green-and-gold study. What good was anything if she couldn't enjoy all the pleasures that had once made her so happy? She put her head down on the desk and drifted into a half sleep. She knew it would leave her feeling worse than before, but she simply didn't have the energy to stop herself.

An hour later, she was still hunched over her desk, her body numb from sitting in the same position for so long, when she heard a knock at the door. Her heart immediately kicked into higher gear at the irrepressible thought that it might be Griff. Of course that was ridiculous, she immediately assured herself. And yet her foolish senses insisted on quickening with interest, the first real sensations she could remember feeling in what seemed like a lifetime.

When she hurried down the stairs she found Velma standing on the other side of the screen door.

"I heard that Griff left a couple of weeks ago," the woman began without preamble, stepping inside the cool dim interior of the house. "I was visiting my daughter. Just got back this morning."

Nickie tried to rouse herself from her self-imposed stupor. "Did you enjoy it?"

"Heck, no. The grandkids acted like a bunch of hooligans the entire time I was there. Still, I love the little devils and it was good to see them, even though I'm plumb wore out." She immediately headed for the salon. "Where he'd go?" she asked, raising her voice to make sure Nickie heard her because she didn't bother turning her head.

"California," Nickie replied, not even flinching at the sudden change of subject. There wasn't much that could rouse her these days. "He has a job there."

They had reached the salon and now Velma did turn around, studying the younger woman's face with a frown. "What's the matter with you? You look as though someone punched out your lights."

Nickie shrugged, one side of her mouth flicking upward in the barest hint of a smile at Velma's colorful language. She just didn't have the energy to try to fool her. She certainly wasn't fooling herself, but then she'd known she'd be hard hit by Griff's departure. She just hadn't known how hard.

"You two had something going between you, didn't you?" Velma nodded, pressing her lips together and nodding her head as she shrewdly looked Nickie over. "Can't say I'm surprised. He's handsome and he's smart, a real catch. Did you fall in love with him?"

"Yes." Nickie sighed. "Yes, I did." Admitting the truth out loud was a relief, although the feeling didn't last long enough to do her any real good.

"Then why are you so down at the mouth? Did he tell you he didn't want to see you again?"

"No. It's just over, that's all."

"Over! It doesn't even sound as if it'd properly begun. Pardon me for being a nosy old woman, but I can't help prying since you look so darn miserable. Could you please explain exactly why it's over?"

"I promised myself the kind of stability a man like Griff could never provide," she replied sadly. "And then of course there's Bellefleur. This house is my responsibility now, one I take very seriously. I can't just wander off whenever I feel like it."

"Bellefleur my foot." Velma rolled her eyes and snorted in disgust. "Don't blame your wishy-washiness on Bellefleur. This house stood empty for over a year after your aunt died with only Tilly Leeds coming in every week to dust and clean. I'm sure it can manage to hang in there for a while more. It's love you can't put on the back burner. Do you expect it to simmer there indefinitely without boiling away?"

Nickie shook her head sorrowfully. "I didn't put it on the back burner," she admitted, her throat muscles tightening. "I turned off the stove completely."

Velma looked at her pityingly. "That's a foolish thing to have done, girl. Especially when you're in love with the man."

There wasn't a whole lot to say after that, so Velma took her leave, clucking her tongue and muttering under her breath as she closed the door behind her.

Not knowing what else to do or where else to go, Nickie wandered listlessly out the front door, her feet automatically taking her along the path that led toward the area of the garden where she and Griff had spent so much time. The afternoon light was rapidly fading, but in spite of the approaching dusk, she could see her way easily enough.

The day Griff had departed, she had come out to the gardens to sit on the marble bench where she'd so recently sketched while watching him work. And she'd cried until she couldn't cry anymore. She'd learned it was best to get all the grief out of her system as soon as possible and get on with her life.

Somehow, this time it hadn't worked. Maybe her life wasn't worth redeeming without Griff, a small inner voice had whispered devilishly. She suddenly couldn't even draw a straight line without his inspiration. He had slipped into the role of her muse and she couldn't seem to dislodge him. Sometimes she wasn't even sure she wanted to. One thing was clear. She couldn't go back to the way things had been when she'd first arrived at Bellefleur.

She'd finally hushed the traitorous voice, but it had returned again and again in the days that followed, and she hadn't been back to the garden since. Strolling along the neatly edged walkway now, she wondered why she'd kept away from what was to her the heart and soul of Bellefleur. The early-evening smells filled her senses and she felt a renewed spark of appreciation for the stunning beauty of life, but it quickly faded, unable to withstand the heavy unhappiness of her soul.

Still, it had been good to experience so she forced her focus outward, away from her own troubles to truly look at the garden Griff had coaxed back to life. The shock of what she saw made her gasp.

It must be the fading light, or more likely her imagination, but she swore the garden had changed, shrunk somehow into something less than it had been only two weeks ago. She blinked and looked again, telling herself to knock it off. But no, the shrubbery was definitely lackluster, dry and somewhat shriveled. And yet she was sure the automatic sprinklers were working—she often heard them come on in the dead of night as she lay quiet and despairing in her bed.

She walked farther along to find that the arabesque of box trees adorned with flowers looked as though a herd of sheep had trampled on it, so flat and lifeless did it appear. Was she dreaming? Hallucinating? She shook her head, but the sorry spectacle didn't go away. She decided that her lousy frame of mind must be coloring her experiences more than she realized. And yet there was no denying that everything looked more bedraggled than when she had first arrived at Bellefleur.

Stunned, she remained rooted to the spot for long minutes, wanting to flee the garden but unable to take the first step. The sweet scent of honeysuckle drifted past her nose on the faint breeze that stirred the leaves of the silver birch trees. There was no moon tonight and the darkness deepened quickly, surrounding and embracing her like the gentlest lover.

She gazed back along the walkway where a white wooden trellis marked the official entrance to the garden, separating it from the original and more ordinary backyard of the house. A sudden movement caught her eye. She gasped again and blinked her eyes, for there stood Audubon.

He was almost invisible in the murky light. She would never have noticed him if he hadn't moved. She watched as he bent over to pick up a limp trailing vine of wisteria, trying in vain to weave it back along the wooden slats that had formerly supported it. Pale purple and pink petals fluttered to the ground as he worked. She could feel his intense concentration.

Had he seen her? Did he know she was there? He must, she thought as she stared at his back. He was always aware of her presence. He paused in his task, his long-fingered hands protectively cupped around one of the blossoms. He usually appeared because he had something to tell her. She wondered what it might be this time.

He finally turned and met her gaze. There was no mistaking the frown on his handsome face as he dropped his arm to his side, letting the vine slide through his ghostly fingertips until it lay like a coiled snake on the ground. He gave her another reproachful look and walked away, dissolving into the soft darkness.

Good grief, even the ghost was angry at her. Nickie covered her face with her hands as if that could keep her emotions in check. It worked for a moment when she squeezed her eyes tightly shut, but when she finally dropped her hands and reopened her eyes it was only to be confronted with that lone wisteria vine, a potent symbol of everything that had gone wrong with her life.

Hot tears welled up in her eyes and spilled down her cheeks. She dashed them away with the back of her hand in frustration and pain, wondering if her life would ever return to its previously cheerful balanced condition. She realized that the garden had become eerily silent without Audubon's presence. The last birds whose calls had punctuated evening's approach had settled down for the night. Everything had become utterly still, but there was no peace associated with it.

As she started walking toward the house the crazy notion entered her head that her showcase garden was losing its luster just the way her life had changed from a limitless technicolor vista to a shadowy black-and-white close-up, with a cropped and unnatural image. The garden was a metaphor of her love for Griff. Without proper nurturing, it would slowly wither and die—just like her heart.

Reeling from the shock of her analogy, she groped her way to the nearest marble bench and sat down.

It was true. Even the motivation and inspiration for her art had vanished. She almost wished she'd never laid eyes on Griff, but that thought was quickly overridden by the remembrance of how he had lifted her beyond the ordinary plane of human existence, as though she were a bird in flight, exhilarated and more alive than she'd ever been before. That wasn't something she could easily forget.

It was as if a particular element had been missing to make her complete, and he had supplied it for her. No wonder they called it chemistry when a man and woman were so right for each other. And she and Griff *were* right for each other, Nickie acknowledged with an aching pain in her chest, in spite of the things that stood between them.

Her pulses fluttered. Was that how he felt about her? Was half of him missing, too, since she'd forced him out of her life?

The thought was more than a little daunting. She lifted her head to glance again at the drooping wisteria. She had to do something, take some kind of action to shake herself out of her misery. Anything was better than this half-life, even if it meant she would only see Griff for the occasional weekend. She simply didn't want to exist anymore without his presence in her world, no matter how infrequent or peripheral.

THE INSIDE of the trailer was ice-cold as the air-conditioning unit hummed steadily in the background. Griff didn't even notice the temperature as he strode past his cluttered desk to snatch up the schematic of the bridge.

"Look, the problem is with the cap plates," Griff explained to Jack Hansford as he stabbed his finger at the drawing.

The foreman had just come in from outside and his face was covered in perspiration. Griff watched impatiently as the man blinked to adjust his eyes to the lesser interior light before walking over to the desk. "Show me, boss," he said.

"See, right here and especially over here. This damn bridge has no structural redundancy. I don't know what the hell the engineers were thinking of, but there's absolutely no backup built into this design, no alternate pathway to carry the load in case of local failure.'' Griff ran an agitated hand through his hair. ''It spells disaster.''

He had to bite his tongue to keep from shouting at the beleaguered supervisor, a fact that had nothing to do with the situation. These jobs were always tense and running behind schedule. Jack Hansford was competent enough, but ever since Griff had arrived here, he'd found his temper on edge. He knew he was a real bear to work with. Although he tried to keep his irritability to a minimum, knowing that no one deserved to suffer from the lash of his sharp tongue, sometimes he couldn't seem to control it.

''The rusting is extensive.'' Griff forced himself to speak in an even nonaccusatory voice. After all, it wasn't the foreman's fault. ''The bridge is weak. We don't want another disaster like the Mianus River Bridge. They were lucky that only three people were killed when it collapsed. It could have been a hell of a lot worse.''

''Yes, sir.''

Griff could see that the man had never heard of the Mianus River Bridge. With a stifled sigh, he waved him to a nearby chair, then began going over how they were going to handle the repairs.

An hour later he was alone in the trailer. It was already after six o'clock and he hadn't had any dinner yet. Come to think of it he'd skipped lunch as well. He pushed himself free from the huge desk that dominated the office and wandered into the small kitchen, which was located in the living area behind the office. Going to the refrigerator, he reached inside for a soda. He popped open the tab and downed half the contents in one long swallow.

He hated this time of the day. Anytime he was alone, he started thinking about things he wanted to forget because they were things that couldn't be changed. An image of Nickie was usually the precursor to the rest of his predictable musings. Sometimes she was sitting on that bench in the garden, so busy sketching that he had ample time to study her. Sometimes she appeared as she had that last morning, naked and tangled in the sheets, her brown eyes soft and sleepy and sated with his lovemaking. It was futile to keep replaying these scenes, but of course he did, going into details that he didn't even particularly notice at the time but that now smugly announced themselves to his consciousness.

When he thought he couldn't stand another minute rehashing all the things he no longer had, his mind would turn to a thorough rundown of what had gone wrong. And from there it was only a short hop to thoughts about what he could do to alter things.

The conclusion to that last aspect was, sadly, always the same. He had asked to be able to continue to see her and she'd said no. That ought to be the end of it. But she was wrong to say no, a little voice inside his head inevitably argued. Yeah, but she'd still said it, he always argued back. He wondered if he should fly to Memphis this weekend and try one more time. After all, it had been two weeks; maybe she had changed her mind. He grimaced at this latest evidence of his irrational thought processes. More likely she had already replaced him with someone else.

Griff shook his head at the image. Now that he was away from the rarified atmosphere of Bellefleur, it all seemed like an enchanted dream. So did Nickie, except she had left him with a broken heart and an aching body that would never forget how sweet she felt in his arms, how satiny her skin when he stroked it or how she had surrounded him in her sweet feminine mystery. That part of it was too real for comfort.

Would he just be torturing himself to go back there again? If he didn't go, he would never know. But dammit, it was up to her to be the one to change things if they were going to be changed. Then again, a man couldn't always trust a woman to carry things through to their logical conclusion. Sometimes they needed help.

He'd give it one more week. He'd left her the phone number at the trailer. He looked around in disgust. Hell, he had actually been living in the place, something he'd never done before on any of his jobs. He'd always gotten himself an apartment or at least a room, but he just hadn't had the interest or the energy this time around. After the unique splendor of Bellefleur, why bother? Besides, remaining here all the time had its advantages. Being bombarded with questions and problems left him less time to think and brood.

He suddenly realized that his skin was icy cold. With a grunt of irritation he got up and turned the thermostat to a more respectable reading, then went outside to warm up.

It was still light outside, although the sun was riding low on the horizon. Men were visible along the south catwalk and beneath the bridge where they were working to provide the extra support needed. It had been necessary to close the bridge to traffic, creating long detours for many commuters, so they were working around the clock on this one.

Griff crumpled the soda can in his fist, deriving a brief moment's satisfaction from the harsh noise the aluminum made as it collapsed beneath his relentless fingers. Anyone watching him as he stood in front of the trailer's sliding glass door would think he was at peace with the world, that he was taking the time to admire the view of the mountains in the distance. The rapidly falling night had tinted their summits a lovely purple rimmed with blue. It was breathtaking.

He heard a wolf whistle somewhere off to his left, but he didn't bother to raise his head to check out the source. He had no desire to contemplate the pros and cons of some unknown female. She wouldn't be able to satisfy his craving for dark wavy hair that managed to be both soft and sassy. She wouldn't have brown eyes he could drown in. He groaned softly. She certainly wouldn't be able to lay claim to her very own ghost.

He shook his head. He must be more brain-dead than he realized if he was waxing nostalgic over that damned spook. When another low whistle sounded, this time accompanied by a hoot of male laughter, he lifted his head to see who was causing the commotion.

A woman stood at the edge of the dirt parking area, her back to him as she spoke to one of the men. Because she had dark brown hair and a slim figure, she immediately reminded him of Nickie. He felt his gut clench in reaction.

She wore a neat little summer dress of yellow that hugged her body in all the right places and left her slender shoulders bare. A small leather purse was tucked under her arm, unlike the usual monstrosities

that many women carted around, able to hold enough
rations to get them and a companion through a minor
siege.

Suddenly the man turned and pointed in Griff's direction. Since they were only fifty yards away Griff
could see the broad smile on the man's face. He
frowned with dawning realization.

When she began walking toward the trailer, he
found himself staring straight into Nickie's face, his
throat working convulsively against this shock to his
system. His eyes flared wider. There could be only one
reason she was here, one reason she had flown all the
way from Tennessee to see him, and it wasn't because
she wanted to be sure he understood it was all over
between them.

He didn't care what provisions she might think she
was going to be able to attach to her presence here or
to how they were going to work out their relationship.
He knew exactly what he was doing, and there was no
room for doubt or second-guessing. They were going
to forge ahead this time, full throttle. She had just
given him permission to do so, simply by showing up.

He watched her for another few seconds, studying
her face, trying to read her expression even as he felt
the smile spread across his face. She looked nervous
and excited and unsure.

She looked beautiful.

''Hello, Griff.''

He closed the short distance between them.
''Nickie.'' It was the faintest whisper of sound, but it
came from his heart.

He pulled her body against his with a small thud,
and then he was hugging her, lifting her off the ground

and squeezing her against him as if he could absorb her very essence into his body. He began dropping kisses on every part of her face and hair he could reach, his hands roaming her body, absorbing the joy of holding her in his arms once again.

"I guess this means you're not mad at me."

"I love you, Nickie," he said against her lips. He couldn't force himself to move any farther away than that. "I'm glad you finally realized I meant it."

His lips sought hers, sliding hotly along her cheek until she lifted her head and he was able to slant his mouth across hers. It was a clumsy kiss because he hardly knew what he was doing but it was the most satisfying one he had ever experienced because in his mind it marked her as his forever.

A handful of sporadic clapping and cheers suddenly broke out, filling the night air. Griff released Nickie, sliding one arm around her shoulders and using the other to acknowledge the cheering workers. And then he urged her toward the trailer.

"They're hoping this means the end of my foul temper," he explained, his eyes meeting the melting warmth of hers for a moment before he pushed open the heavy glass door and ushered her inside.

He slid the door closed behind them. "Come here," he growled.

He barely managed to restrain himself long enough to lead her to the back of the trailer and away from the revealing glass. The only thing keeping him from ravishing her on the spot was the need for enough privacy that they wouldn't be interrupted again. Not that any of the men would dare come here now, not if they valued their lives.

He pulled her up against him again, his lower body hard with desire. "Marry me, Nickie. Marry me, and then you'll have to let me work things out. And I promise I will. Whatever it takes."

Before she could catch her breath long enough to answer, he was kissing her again. She didn't protest. He realized that she still had the purse clutched under one arm, so he reached to take it from her, letting it drop to the floor by their feet. All he knew was that she was kissing him back with everything in her, a totally satisfying form of greeting as far as he was concerned and one that needed no change in course. He decided he would require plenty more of it while he assuaged two empty weeks without her.

"Oh, Griff," she said on a sigh when he finally drew back to catch his breath. Her lips curved in a tremulous smile.

But he was too agitated to return it. The surface of his need for her had barely been scratched. All he could think about was fusing himself and Nickie together, the sooner the better. He scooped her up in his arms and carried her to the rumpled bed.

"There's no turning back now," he told her softly as he studied the yellow dress for a brief moment to discover the quickest way of removing it. It had a zipper up the back and he immediately reached for the tab. "Your fate has been signed, sealed and delivered to me."

"In person," she whispered in agreement. "I love you, Griff."

Her words released the final bit of restraint he'd been clinging to out of some misguided notion he mustn't go too quickly for her. He realized none of those barriers existed anymore. He was free to love her the way he wanted to love her, without holding anything back for fear he would overwhelm her. She loved him, she had just told him so, and that made her his forever.

He tossed the dress in the vague direction of a nearby chair. He hoped she wouldn't be upset by his cavalier treatment of it, but his mind was preoccupied by other, more important matters. Hell, he'd buy her a hundred dresses if it made her happy. And delicate silky slips too, he vowed as he removed the sexy lacy little confection she wore beneath the dress.

Only when she was finally naked and lying against the pillows did he kneel next to her and begin pulling his shirt and pants from his body. He was barely aware of the physical motions of flinging the items away, and he certainly had no idea where they landed. All he could do was stare at Nickie, his gaze taking in the hot look in her eyes as she watched him and the restless movements of her body against the sheets as she waited impatiently for him to come to her.

He didn't allow her to suffer his absence long. Quickly he lowered himself along her body, savoring every new contact of his flesh against hers until he had covered her completely. Nickie's arms welcomed him as she held him tightly and her legs wrapped around his. He knew it wouldn't take much more to send him over the edge. He should inform her that she was playing with forces beyond his control here, that he wouldn't be able to love her the way she should be loved if she kept it up. But it felt so good he wasn't sure if he was heroic enough to do so.

"Nickie!" He blurted out her name on a surge of pleasure as he exhaled the breath he'd been unconsciously holding. It was meant to be a warning. He knew he was only hanging on through sheer willpower, which threatened to give out at any minute, but she apparently didn't get the message as she continued kissing his face. Her hands seemed to be all over his body and the sensations she aroused when she stroked and caressed his skin were indescribable.

When she squeezed him between her thighs, his lungs began pumping air like a winded runner. "Sweetheart," he gasped, "I don't think I can wait for you this time. I can barely wait for myself."

"I'm glad I'm not the only one," she whispered. "I want to drive you so crazy you can't think straight."

"It's too late for that." He tried to chuckle but it came out ragged. "I haven't been able to think straight since I met you."

He felt her reach down between their bodies, her fingers wrapping around him and gently guiding him, and he knew it was all over, especially when she whispered, "I want what you want."

"Oh, God," he moaned as he felt himself slip easily inside. "It's so good, so..." His voice trailed off into another moan as pure instinct took over and he began a rhythmic thrusting.

He was wrong about leaving Nickie behind. She was with him every step of the way, their minds and emotions as joined as their bodies. He could feel the pressure building in his lower body just as he sensed it in hers. The pleasure expanded until it filled the bed, wrapping around them and lifting them to the pinnacle of human experience.

Suddenly the turbulent mass of emotion and sensation that they had built to such a crescendo became too large for either of them to control. Nickie came hurtling back to earth first, her soft cries filling his ears as the essence of everything she meant to him filled his senses to overflowing. He followed her shortly afterward, diving headlong from such an impossible height he wasn't sure a mortal being could survive the pleasure of the landing. He knew he would never be the same again.

He was barely conscious, but he managed to shift some of his weight off to one side to avoid crushing her. If she felt as boneless and contented as he did, he wasn't sure she would particularly care about such a mundane matter. His entire body was slick with sweat. The upper half, especially his back, was rapidly cooling in the faint breeze from the air conditioner while the lucky areas of flesh that remained pressed against Nickie's warm skin were still generating enough local heat to give him ideas about starting all over again.

The minutes passed as he remained sprawled across her, his legs entangled with hers and his face buried in her sweet-smelling hair. Some of the strands tickled his nose, but he didn't have the energy to brush them aside. Besides, he enjoyed the feathery sensation.

Finally the cool breeze across his buttocks convinced him it was time to push his legs beneath the sheets. He shifted to his side, sliding Nickie against him, then pulling the blanket up until it covered them.

"Mmm, nice," she murmured as she wrapped her arms around his where they held her and snuggled her bottom closer. He could have sworn he was totally sated, yet his body tightened in response.

"I don't think this bed can compare in the romance department to that antique four-poster at Bellefleur," he said.

"I don't know about that. As soon as that antique four-poster at Bellefleur lost you, its romantic value plummeted to rock bottom." She turned her head so she could look at him over her shoulder. She was grinning. "You don't really believe I'm such a snob as all that, do you?"

"Not if you invite me to come live with you in your enchanted house." He took in her widened eyes and surprised expression and laughed. "To be quite honest, this gypsy existence of mine is beginning to lose its appeal. I'm getting tired of take-out food and lumpy beds like this one."

"What's this!" she exclaimed, her eyes sparkling. She wriggled around in his arms until she was facing him. "And here I was just thinking that I missed the excitement of seeing new places and meeting new people."

"So, we'll work something out." He kissed her gently on the mouth. "What changed your mind?"

She grinned as a teasing light danced in her eyes. "I had to save the garden."

"Save the garden?" He grabbed both her hands and rolled her onto her back, pinning her arms next to her head as he glared ominously down at her. She didn't seem at all alarmed. "What are you talking about? I already saved your garden before I left." He moved his lower body until that held her down, too.

Nickie squirmed a bit as if to test the limits of his strength, and then subsided against the pillows with another grin. "That's true, you did. In more ways than one."

"What do you mean?"

"Well, you restored the vegetation with your physical labor by actually weeding and trimming and all that. And then you made it blossom spiritually, through your love for me." She lowered her gaze for an introspective moment. "When I sent you away everything started sliding into another decline."

"You're kidding." He shook his head as he pondered her words.

"You don't sound very surprised."

"I'm not. The morning after we made love for the first time I went into the garden. Remember how the flower beds showed more dirt than plant?"

She nodded.

"All the bare spots were filled in. I thought I was dreaming, but the more I stared at it, the more lush it seemed to become, until I thought I really had wandered into Versailles. It was as if every plant had grown during the night at an uncanny rate. At the time I put it down to my imagination."

"It wasn't your imagination. Everything started deteriorating at the same rate as soon as you left. I thought I was going crazy, too, but it's true. If a garden can look unhappy, that one did. Even Audubon was mad at me for letting you go."

He released her wrists, shifting his weight to his elbows so he could frame her face with his hands. All the tenderness he felt for her went into the gesture. "Bellefleur is a house that needs someone to love it. It also seems to thrive on having people within its walls who love each other."

"Is this your subtle way of telling me you wouldn't mind living there?"

"I want us to be together, Nickie. If you don't mind an interloper in your fairy-tale palace, I'd be honored to live there with you. But I'm going to need some help to make it come true."

She brushed the dark hair back from his forehead with loving fingers. "Name it."

"What do you think about hitting the road with me for a while, just until I can figure out a way to stay at Bellefleur and earn a living at the same time. Do you think your roots will stretch as far as California?"

"They already have." Her smile was brilliant as she reached up to kiss him.

His eyes flared with instant heat in response to her gesture. He wanted her again and as proof his body surged against her. Nickie drew a quick breath and held it, her gaze locking with his for a timeless moment as the world stood still. He could see that she approved of the idea. He pressed her down into the mattress again, just to test her resilience before he spoke again. Once he finished with everything he wanted to tell her, she was going to find herself even more thoroughly ravished than the first time. He had his wits about him now, and he intended to pleasure her until she cried uncle.

"I have to finish up here before we make any serious plans. But we could return to Bellefleur for a couple of long weekends in the meantime. Do you think the plants and flowers will get the message that everything's going to be all right and make a comeback?"

"Why not?" She rolled her eyes. "They certainly knew right away when everything went wrong."

He shifted his weight to one elbow using his free hand to cover her breast. He watched her eyes darken as he allowed his palm to rub the crest with just enough pressure to make her want more. "As long as your ghost knows when he's not wanted, we should do okay."

She reached up to slide her fingers into his thick dark hair, pulling his head down. "He's a gentleman, not a voyeur," she said on a soft moan as she pressed herself to his mouth.

He didn't need a second invitation.

# Epilogue

It was hard to believe that six months had passed since she'd flown out to California, Nickie thought with a smile as she studied her simple wedding band. She lifted her eyes to gaze at the shimmering green-and-gold elegance of her study at Bellefleur, thinking she might explode from sheer happiness. They'd only arrived a couple of days ago, but it had been blissfully easy to adjust to Bellefleur's gracious accommodations although Griff had assured her he would never adjust to the bathroom.

She glanced at the top of the desk where a stack of books and her art supplies were piled. No wonder the house seemed so happy. She'd been commissioned by the National Historical Society to do the illustrations for a book about Bellefleur's unique history, which was also to include the new information about Audubon's origins.

Griff had started his job as an inspector for the city of Memphis only yesterday, and he seemed to like it. His main intention, however, was to begin a free-lance consulting business, something that would allow him the space and growth potential he needed to feel fulfilled, yet allow him to remain by her side.

Velma had been right. She didn't have to be at Bellefleur every hour of the day to love it and care for it or even to have her roots there. She could always come back, just as she had returned this time, several months later. She even had to admit that the return had been all the sweeter for the time spent away. She must be more of a vagabond at heart than she'd imagined.

"Nickie!"

Her smile widened to the breaking point. She hadn't heard his car pull up, but then, after the trip back from California he had spent an entire day tuning it, so it was no wonder.

"Up here!" she called out.

When she heard his footsteps on the steps, she braced herself for the fifth one to creak. She wasn't disappointed. Seconds later Griff ambled into the room as if he hadn't just dashed up the stairs at full speed.

"Hi," he said. His eyes were already gleaming with that special look she knew, the one that told her he wasn't interested in conversation or dinner or describing his day.

He had already removed his jacket. He now reached for the knot of his tie, giving it a sharp tug until it loosened and then pulling it free from his collar. He tossed it over a nearby chair and walked toward her.

"Did you make the bed today?" he asked, pulling her out of her seat and taking her into his arms.

"Of course."

He kissed her, hard and fast, a promise of more to come. "Good. Then let's go unmake it."

"You must have had a pleasant day."

"I don't remember. The only thing on my mind since I passed the city limits was you."

He released her long enough to urge her toward the door. She slipped her arm around his waist and gave him a hug, although nothing could express the sheer happiness that filled every fiber of her being. They stepped into the hallway together.

And there he was.

Nickie let out a small gasp as her gaze took in the sight of Audubon, hovering anxiously about twenty feet away. He was dressed as if to go out, in a handsome overcoat that sported a shoulder cape of the sort Sherlock Holmes wore. He carried a hat and a pair of brown leather gloves in one hand and an elegant walking stick with a gold handle in the other.

"What the hell . . ." Griff's voice trailed off as the ghost slanted him a reproachful glare. Probably for his language in front of a lady, Nickie thought with a faint giggle. Then the shock of what he was seeing finally began to register. She felt Griff's arm fall to his side as he stood rooted to the floor, staring. Nickie knew exactly how he felt.

Audubon sketched a grudging bow in Griff's direction. Then he turned to Nickie and kissed his hand at her, his gaze soft and affectionate.

"Oh!" she said as the implications of what he was doing dawned on her. "You're not going away?"

He made another gesture as if to touch her face, his eloquent features expressing his regret. After another bow, he put on the tall-crowned top hat, tapping it to a jaunty angle on his head. His eyes gleamed out at her from beneath the shallow curled brim for a long time-less moment, and then he turned and began walking away.

She felt a lump in her throat as she watched him dissolve. He had come to say goodbye, after all. She had the feeling that this time it was permanent. She reached out and clasped Griff's hand in hers.

He gripped it hard in return. "Damn," he muttered. "I know what I just saw, but I still don't believe it."

She gave his arm a sharp tug. "What do you mean, you don't believe it? Haven't I been telling you about him all along?"

"Sure." Griff turned his bemused gaze on her. "But it's not the same thing as actually seeing him, is it?"

"No, it's not the same thing at all."

"Why?"

She understood immediately what he was asking. "My best guess is that, since we're married, he must now consider you part of the family."

Griff chuckled. "It didn't thrill him to acknowledge me."

"Why should it when the first thing out of your mouth was a swear word?"

"A rather mild one."

"Not to him."

Several minutes of thoughtful quiet passed before Griff spoke again. "Somehow I think that was his final farewell."

Nickie nodded in sad agreement. "Yes, it looks that way. Do you suppose he's going somewhere in particular?"

"Like where?"

"I don't know. Maybe he has other houses he's supposed to haunt."

Griff laughed. "Let's hope the poor guy doesn't have to work so hard the next time around to get his point across."

"Can you never be serious about these things?" she asked, poking him in the ribs. "That was a very poignant moment we just experienced."

"I'll allow you to handle the poignant aspects involved in the matter. I was just plain shocked."

"You must have been. You didn't even return his bow."

He sketched one in her direction now. "I never said I was much of a gentleman."

"I know and I'm glad. Too much politeness can get to you after a while."

Griff smiled wryly. "It's so nice for a man to be loved as he really is, warts and all."

She chuckled at his droll expression, then immediately returned to the subject of the ghost. "That must have been his purpose—to inform the world of his origins. He must have regretted not telling anybody the truth about his birth, although the Clermonts must have known."

"And also Audubon's wife. Don't you remember?" Griff said when he saw her puzzled frown. "She threw herself on their son's casket during his funeral crying, 'My son, my son, to think I never told you who you are,' or words to that effect. It was all in that 'dubious' biography, which turned out to be not so dubious, after all."

"Of course." She blew out her breath. "Do you think he'll miss Bellefleur?"

"I'm sure he will. Didn't we?"

She smiled softly at his generous wording. It implied that they had both missed the place equally, although she was sure that wasn't the case. "Yes," she agreed, her eyes shining, "we did."

"I hate to change the subject." He took her by the hand, gently pulling her toward their original destination. "But we were right in the middle of extremely urgent business when we were rudely interrupted."

When he arrived by the side of the huge four-poster he lifted her in his arms and sat her on the edge of the mattress. "Do you know why none of this matters?" he asked as he nudged her thighs apart so he could step into their welcoming circle.

She shook her head.

"Because we don't need his magic anymore. Or anyone else's, for that matter. We have enough of our own to last a lifetime."

And it was true. With only a little assistance from a ghost and a garden, the magic of their love had overcome every obstacle.

Fifty red-blooded, white-hot, true-blue hunks
from every State in the Union!

Look for MEN MADE IN AMERICA! Written by some
of our most poplar authors, these stories feature fifty of
the strongest, sexiest men, each from a different state in
the union!

Two titles available every other month at your favorite
retail outlet.

In March, look for:

TANGLED LIES by Anne Stuart (Hawaii)
ROGUE'S VALLEY by Kathleen Creighton (Idaho)

In May, look for:

LOVE BY PROXY by Diana Palmer (Illinois)
POSSIBLES by Lass Small (Indiana)

**You won't be able to resist MEN MADE IN AMERICA!**

If you missed your state or would like to order any other states that have already been published, send your name, address, zip or postal code along with a check or money order (please
do not send cash) for $3.59 for each book, plus 75¢ postage and handling ($1.00 in Canada),
payable to Harlequin Reader Service, to:

| In the U.S. | In Canada |
|---|---|
| 3010 Walden Avenue | P.O. Box 609 |
| P.O. Box 1369 | Fort Erie, Ontario |
| Buffalo, NY 14269-1369 | L2A 5X3 |

Please specify book title(s) with your order.
Canadian residents add applicable federal and provincial taxes.                    MEN394

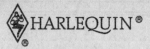

### HARLEQUIN®

## COMING SOON TO
## A STORE NEAR YOU...

# THE MAIN
# ATTRACTION

By *New York Times* Bestselling Author

This March, look for THE MAIN ATTRACTION by popular
author Jayne Ann Krentz.

Ten years ago, Filomena Cromwell had left her small town
in shame. Now she is back determined to get her sweet,
sweet revenge....

Soon she has her ex-fiancé, who cheated on her with
another woman, chasing her all over town. And he isn't
the only one. Filomena lets Trent Ravinder catch her.

Can she control the fireworks she's set into motion?

BOB8

## THE BABY IS ADORABLE...
## BUT WHICH MAN IS HIS DADDY?

*Alec Roman:* He found baby Andy in a heart-shaped Valentine basket—but were finders necessarily keepers?

*Jack Rourke:* During his personal research into Amish culture, he got close to an Amish beauty—so close he thought he was the father.

*Grady Noland:* The tiny bundle of joy softened this rogue cop—and made him want to own up to what he thought were his responsibilities.

Cathy Gillen Thacker brings you TOO MANY DADS, a three-book series that asks the all-important question: Which man is about to become a daddy?

**Meet the potential fathers in:**
**#521 BABY ON THE DOORSTEP**
**February 1994**
**#526 DADDY TO THE RESCUE**
**March 1994**
**#529 TOO MANY MOMS**
**April 1994**

If you missed any titles in this miniseries, here's your chance to order them:

| | | | |
|---|---|---|---|
| #521 | BABY ON THE DOORSTEP | $3.50 | ☐ |
| #526 | DADDY TO THE RESCUE | $3.50 | ☐ |

| | |
|---|---|
| **TOTAL AMOUNT** | $ |
| **POSTAGE & HANDLING** | $ |
| ($1.00 for one book, 50¢ for each additional) | |
| **APPLICABLE TAXES\*** | $ _____ |
| <u>**TOTAL PAYABLE**</u> | $ _____ |
| (check or money order—please do not send cash) | |

To order, complete this form and send it, along with a check or money order for the total above, payable to Harlequin Books, to: *In the U.S.:* 3010 Walden Avenue, P.O. Box 9047, Buffalo, NY 14269-9047; *In Canada:* P.O. Box 613, Fort Erie, Ontario, L2A 5X3.

Name: _____

Address: _____ City: _____

State/Prov.: _____ Zip/Postal Code: _____

\*New York residents remit applicable sales taxes.
 Canadian residents remit applicable GST and provincial taxes.

DADS2

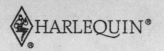

Harlequin proudly presents four stories about *convenient* but not *conventional* reasons for marriage:

- ◆ To save your godchildren from a "wicked stepmother"

- ◆ To help out your eccentric aunt—and her sexy business partner

- ◆ To bring an old man happiness by making him a grandfather

- ◆ To escape from a ghostly existence and become a real woman

Marriage By Design—four brand-new stories by four of Harlequin's most popular authors:

**CATHY GILLEN THACKER**
**JASMINE CRESSWELL**
**GLENDA SANDERS**
**MARGARET CHITTENDEN**

Don't miss this exciting collection of stories about marriages of convenience. Available in April, wherever Harlequin books are sold.

MBD94

**HARLEQUIN®**

Don't miss these Harlequin favorites by some of our most distin-
guished authors!
And now, you can receive a discount by ordering two or more titles!

| | | | |
|---|---|---|---|
| HT#25409 | THE NIGHT IN SHINING ARMOR by JoAnn Ross | $2.99 | ☐ |
| HT#25471 | LOVESTORM by JoAnn Ross | $2.99 | ☐ |
| HP#11463 | THE WEDDING by Emma Darcy | $2.89 | ☐ |
| HP#11592 | THE LAST GRAND PASSION by Emma Darcy | $2.99 | ☐ |
| HR#03188 | DOUBLY DELICIOUS by Emma Goldrick | $2.89 | ☐ |
| HR#03248 | SAFE IN MY HEART by Leigh Michaels | $2.89 | ☐ |
| HS#70464 | CHILDREN OF THE HEART by Sally Garrett | $3.25 | ☐ |
| HS#70524 | STRING OF MIRACLES by Sally Garrett | $3.39 | ☐ |
| HS#70500 | THE SILENCE OF MIDNIGHT by Karen Young | $3.39 | ☐ |
| HI#22178 | SCHOOL FOR SPIES by Vickie York | $2.79 | ☐ |
| HI#22212 | DANGEROUS VINTAGE by Laura Pender | $2.89 | ☐ |
| HI#22219 | TORCH JOB by Patricia Rosemoor | $2.89 | ☐ |
| HAR#16459 | MACKENZIE'S BABY by Anne McAllister | $3.39 | ☐ |
| HAR#16466 | A COWBOY FOR CHRISTMAS by Anne McAllister | $3.39 | ☐ |
| HAR#16462 | THE PIRATE AND HIS LADY by Margaret St. George | $3.39 | ☐ |
| HAR#16477 | THE LAST REAL MAN by Rebecca Flanders | $3.39 | ☐ |
| HH#28704 | A CORNER OF HEAVEN by Theresa Michaels | $3.99 | ☐ |
| HH#28707 | LIGHT ON THE MOUNTAIN by Maura Seger | $3.99 | ☐ |

### Harlequin Promotional Titles

| | | | |
|---|---|---|---|
| #83247 | YESTERDAY COMES TOMORROW by Rebecca Flanders | $4.99 | ☐ |
| #83257 | MY VALENTINE 1993 | $4.99 | ☐ |
| | (short-story collection featuring Anne Stuart, Judith Arnold, Anne McAllister, Linda Randall Wisdom) | | |

**(limited quantities available on certain titles)**

| | | |
|---|---|---|
| | AMOUNT | $ |
| DEDUCT: | 10% DISCOUNT FOR 2+ BOOKS | $ |
| ADD: | POSTAGE & HANDLING | $ |
| | ($1.00 for one book, 50¢ for each additional) | |
| | APPLICABLE TAXES* | $ _____ |
| | TOTAL PAYABLE | $ _____ |
| | (check or money order—please do not send cash) | |

To order, complete this form and send it, along with a check or money order for the
total above, payable to Harlequin Books, to: **In the U.S.:** 3010 Walden Avenue,
P.O. Box 9047, Buffalo, NY 14269-9047; **In Canada:** P.O. Box 613, Fort Erie, Ontario,
L2A 5X3.

Name: _____

Address: _____ City: _____

State/Prov.: _____ Zip/Postal Code: _____

*New York residents remit applicable sales taxes.
Canadian residents remit applicable GST and provincial taxes.

HBACK-JM

## When the only time you have for yourself is…

STOLEN moments

*Spring* into spring—by giving yourself a March Break! Take a few *stolen moments* and treat yourself to a Great Escape. Relax with one of our brand-new stories (or with all six!).

Each STOLEN MOMENTS title in our Great Escapes collection is a complete and never-before-published *short* novel. These contemporary romances are 96 pages long—the perfect length for the busy woman of the nineties!

### Look for Great Escapes in our Stolen Moments display this March!

SIZZLE  by Jennifer Crusie
ANNIVERSARY WALTZ
by Anne Marie Duquette
MAGGIE AND HER COLONEL
by Merline  Lovelace
PRAIRIE SUMMER by Alina Roberts
THE SUGAR CUP by Annie Sims
LOVE ME NOT by Barbara Stewart

### Wherever Harlequin and Silhouette books are sold.

SMGE

### HARLEQUIN® AMERICAN ROMANCE®

Meet four of the most mysterious, magical men in

### MORE THAN MEN

These men are more than tall, dark and handsome. They have extraordinary powers that make them "more than men." But whether they are able to grant you three wishes, communicate with dolphins or live forever, make no mistake—their greatest, most extraordinary power is of seduction.

Make a date with all these MORE THAN MEN:

| | | | |
|---|---|---|---|
| #501 | A WISH…AND A KISS by Margaret St. George | $3.50 | ☐ |
| #509 | NEPTUNE'S BRIDE by Anne Marie Duquette | $3.50 | ☐ |
| #517 | FOREVER ALWAYS by Rebecca Flanders | $3.50 | ☐ |
| #525 | CINDERMAN by Anne Stuart | $3.50 | ☐ |

**(limited quantities available on certain titles)**

| | |
|---|---|
| **TOTAL AMOUNT** | $ |
| **POSTAGE & HANDLING** | $ |
| ($1.00 for one book, 50¢ for each additional) | |
| **APPLICABLE TAXES\*** | $ _____ |
| **TOTAL PAYABLE** | $ _____ |
| (check or money order—please do not send cash) | |

To order, complete this form and send it, along with a check or money order for the total above, payable to Harlequin Books, to: **In the U.S.:** 3010 Walden Avenue, P.O. Box 9047, Buffalo, NY 14269-9047; **In Canada:** P.O. Box 613, Fort Erie, Ontario, L2A 5X3.

Name: _____
Address: _____ City: _____
State/Prov.: _____ Zip/Postal Code: _____

\*New York residents remit applicable sales taxes.
 Canadian residents remit applicable GST and provincial taxes.

MTMORDER